The Far Away Home

Marci Denesiuk

NEWEST PRESS

Library and Archives Canada Cataloguing in Publication
Denesiuk, Marci, 1969-
The far away home / Marci Denesiuk.

(Nunatak fiction)
Short stories.
Originally published as the author's thesis (M.A.-Concordia), 2000.
ISBN 1-896300-79-0

I. Title. II. Series.

PS8557.E557F37 2005   C813'.6   C2004-906667-6

Editor: Dave Margoshes
Cover design: Andree-Ann Thievierge
Cover image: Gigi Perron
Author photograph: Claudio Calligaris

Author's acknowledgements: I am deeply grateful to my family and friends, especially Tally Abecassis, Shaughnessy Bishop-Stall, Catherine Bodmer, Benoît Chaput, Cheryl Crane, Richard Deschênes, Eric Duceppe, Jane Jackel, Karl Jarosiewicz, Ibi Kaslik, Nancy Liknes, Meghan Price, Eric Smith, John Schweitzer, and Leah Weinberg. Special thanks go to Sean Locke for his encouragement, patience, and instruction in ground-fighting. I am also hugely grateful to Terence Byrnes and Dave Margoshes for their editorial guidance and unwavering support.

 Canada Council   Conseil des Arts
for the Arts   du Canada

 Canadian   Patrimoine
Heritage   canadien

NeWest Press acknowledges the support of the Canada Council for the Arts and the Alberta Foundation for the Arts, and the Edmonton Arts Council for our publishing program. We also acknowledge the financial support of the Government of Canada through the Book Publishing Industry Development Program (BPIDP) for our activities.

NeWest Press
201–8540–109 Street
Edmonton, Alberta T6G 1E6
(780) 432-9427
www.newestpress.com

1 2 3 4 5 08 07 06 05

PRINTED AND BOUND IN CANADA

For my parents,

Ruth and Russell Denesiuk,

and my sister, Lisa

Ladybug, Ladybug, fly away home.
Your house is on fire, your children are alone.

Table of Contents

Pieces

*In a million pieces the chance of having certain
moments increases.* —Scrawl

"Is that it?" the doctor asks, head between Jody's legs, finger pressing down, searching.

"I'm not sure. I think so." She shifts ever so slightly in the stirrups. Her movement is not so much a result of physical discomfort, as it is a sign to the doctor that Jody knows his is not a fun job, that she, too, takes no pleasure having him pry into her private parts. The doctor responds sympathetically; he keeps the conversation impersonal, medical.

"It's not really on the lips is it? It's more towards your buttocks. Is that where you were talking about?"

"I'm not sure. It's kind of small. Ummm, maybe if I could just . . ." Jody laughs an embarrassed little snort as she reaches her hand over the paper blanket. Her face gets hot with the thought of touching herself in front of a stranger. It doesn't help that he's young, has good teeth and steady eyes.

"Ummm . . . yeah . . . I think . . . I think that's it there. It's gotten smaller. I think that's where you were?" Jody feels the doctor's gloved finger next to hers, probing.

"There?"

"Yeah, there."

"That's not a wart, that's a pimple."

"Oh."

"Well, that's good news anyway." The doctor rolls back on his chair and snaps off his gloves. "Warts are white cauliflower-like growths. The bump you have is red. Was there pus in it?"

Jody squirms. "I don't know. I really couldn't see."

"It looks like the head was scratched open. Is it sore?"

Jody cringes, wondering if this is his discreet way of suggesting she squeezed the pimple on her butt. She repeats herself, trying to reinforce the idea that she doesn't generally have her hands down there a lot. "It's hard to see. It's not really sore at all."

"If you take a mirror and sit in good light you usually can get a better look. When was your last contact with this partner?" Jody explained earlier that her ex had the virus and that they faithfully used condoms—except for one night. One night and she got pregnant, and ever since she's been expecting something else to go wrong.

"It's been a while."

The doctor moves around to Jody's side. "The chance of contracting the virus after being exposed once is about 30 per cent. If it hasn't appeared within a few months after contact, then you can be sure you're safe. I've taken a pap smear and I'll get them to run the gonorrhea/yeast/chlamydia tests. Your ovaries seem fine and your uterus is small." Jody doesn't know why, but for some reason she feels proud. It just seems tidier to have a small uterus.

"I'll do a breast examination now." As she feels the cover being pulled down and tucked around her waist, Jody stares at the ceiling. His breath smells like Juicy Fruit with a lingering hint of cigarettes. She concentrates on the poster hanging above her. A whale is jumping out of the water, trying to reach a small sardine on the end of the trainer's long stick. It reminds her of the one visit she made to the Vancouver Aquarium before she moved to the west coast.

It was ten years ago. After graduation, she and her best friend, William, drove to Vancouver for a weekend to see the Police in concert. On a Sunday afternoon, before heading back to Calgary, they stopped in Stanley Park for the dolphin show. They were both severely hungover. The bright sun stabbed Jody's eyes and her back hurt from sitting in the stands. But when the dolphins jumped and splashed water on the audience,

William and Jody both lifted their faces to welcome the cool, salty spray against their hot cheeks.

"Do you like my whale picture?" The profile of the doctor's head is indistinct as Jody keeps her gaze fixed on the ceiling.

"HmmMmm," she affirms, thinking about how cold his hands are. The doctor pulls up the blanket and reports that everything seems fine. He turns his back on Jody's nodding head and disappears behind the curtain.

Hastily pulling on her jeans and T-shirt, she looks down at her outfit and thinks she's dressed like someone who would have an abortion. Jody can't believe that after seven months she still feels self-conscious. She draws back the curtain and sits by the desk, her legs pressed closely together, her bag pushed tightly into her lap. As the doctor fills in a chart, Jody's eyes wander over the shelves, taking inventory of what she might like to have, what she could take from this place if she had a chance. She likes the tongue depressors. An oxygen tank with a mask would come in handy for her panic attacks, but Jody doesn't spot one.

The doctor stops writing and rests his hands on her open file. "I see you've been to this medi-centre a few times since the procedure you had last fall, checking up on some minor concerns like today." His eyes aren't accusing, his voice merely inquiring, but Jody inspects the floor thoroughly, as if seeking an escape hatch. "How do you feel about the abortion?" the doctor breaks the silence.

Jody tells him what she has told everyone who knows to ask, "I feel OK."

"You're not suicidal?"

"No."

"No regrets?"

"No."

She is telling the truth. She's known for a long time that if she ever got pregnant she would get rid of the baby. These words—pregnant and baby—seem strange to her. At first, Jody referred to her pregnancy as "the invasion" and the baby was "an enemy." She toyed with the idea of possession, but soon realized that this was no otherworldly affair—it was a war for territory. Later, she refused to discuss the abortion, but in her mind she renamed the baby "my visitor." Her unwanted houseguest.

"How many weeks were you?"

"Seven," she replies and remembers how much longer it seemed, the sleeping days and sleepless nights.

The doctor nods once, the answer is acceptable.

"I'm really fine." Jody wants to convince this doctor that his duty has been done. "My friend just had a baby and I'm really happy for her. They've named her Seraphina. Reminds me of serendipity."

Another nod. "I'm giving you a sheet with the tests I've done today. You can call for the results in two weeks." Jody takes the paper, folds it in half and stashes it in her bag. She doesn't want to see the list of tests that will be run on a part of her, out there, separate.

As she leaves the room, Jody tosses a "thank you" behind her. She passes the reception desk and escapes. The bright sun is an insult to her mood and she's happy when it disappears behind a wall of thick, fast-moving clouds.

She has about an hour before she has to be at work, just enough time to grab a quick bite and stop by home for her apron. She picks up a ready-made sandwich and quickly moves through downtown towards her nearby neighbour-hood. Victoria's centre is so little she can easily walk or ride her bicycle everywhere. This was one of the attractions when she decided to move west after high school. Unfortunately, the small-town atmosphere also included a certain reticence towards strangers. After a decade, she still has few friends.

There is only Sal. Sal of the genital warts. Sal of the abor-tion.

Sal eats fire. He juggles it, blows it, tosses it high in the air and swallows it. Jody had first seen him in the market square doing his fire act for tourists. Three years ago, when she got the job at the deli, there he was again, wearing a hair net and plastic gloves. "Fire pays," he said when she asked him if he were still busking. "But not enough."

Soon after, Sal and Jody became what he called "fuck buddies." When he came to her bed, he smelled like kerosene. His kisses tasted burnt, charred. She felt he was too young for her. He had too much energy. The difference between twenty and twenty-eight can be great. He was always urging her to *do* something. "How can you work at these shit jobs and not give yourself time to be creative? Paint! Draw! Write! Act! Sing!" When he pushed too hard, she told him to leave her alone, she was happy with her sliced turkey and blood sausage.

She'd never really had ambition. Even in high school, while others joined drama clubs and sports teams or excelled in English or math, she'd always hung back, an average student with no interest in anything except smoking joints and listening to music. Dark circles ringed her bloodshot eyes and earphones constantly crowned her head. She was easily overlooked.

Jody quickly passes the deli now. The volume on her Walkman turned up high, she keeps her eyes fixed in front of her. She knows Sal is also working there today and she will see him soon enough. She turns the corner onto a residential street and pauses to look out over the little man-made lake only a few blocks from her house. The shore is lined with tall reeds and the water is covered with a layer of dark sludge. When the loons swim, the algae collects on their white breast feathers, staining them a dark green that matches their heads. Jody walks out onto the pier where people sit and throw bread to the birds. She plops down and unwraps her ham and cheese.

William would call this lake a puddle, but Jody likes it. She even prefers it to the ocean. The pond makes her think of Jackfish Lake and long summer days spent with William on the pier in front of his parents' cabin. When they were kids he used to dangle her off the edge, threatening to let her fall into the water. And even though Jody spent hours swimming and diving into that same water, she nervously pleaded with William to hold onto her, to not let her go.

William continued this practice through the years, but never once dropped her. Even when she grew tall and lanky, he always managed to pull her back and lay her down on the dock. Her heart still pounding, her armpits wet, she stretched her long legs, wiggled her toes and listened to the water quietly slapping the boards of the deck. William sat beside her, stroking her head. His fingers were rough and snagged her hair, but every time he moved his arm Jody smelled the sun on his skin. During these times, William often reached into his pocket to take out a bottle of small white pills, shaking one or two into the palm of his hand. The medication was prescribed to calm him and silence the voices he sometimes heard. William never talked about his problem and the sight of him chewing pills became familiar.

Jody has thought a lot about William lately. It happens sometimes that she can spend days in the past. She remembers William's history of scarring himself with small, precise cuts along his arms and legs. He said the pain helped him to focus, to escape his head and come back into his body. Jody was used to the trail of scabs covering William's skin. She grew comfortable seeing him with a knife.

One day, she picked up his blade and started to chisel faces into a piece of wood. Each side showed a different expression: one smiled with its eyes shut, one seemed to snarl or sneer, and one opened its mouth in terror. William insisted on keeping the sculpture, convinced it was a portrait of him. The next day he gave her his knife and stopped cutting himself. Jody began carving out of a superstitious belief that her actions could somehow protect her friend and stopped carving when she was proven wrong again and again as William found new ways to hurt himself. She did keep his knife, though, and used it to cut parts from trees, plastic chairs, driftwood, dolls—anything that felt good in the palm of her hand. Rough, smooth, solid, soft. She'd stroke these pieces and remember.

Before, when she was overcome by nostalgia, she called William. She used to think her sudden recollections of him were a sign and she needed to know that he was fine. Every time she called, he not only assured her he was fine, but also expressed surprise at her concern. Now she rarely phoned him. The last time was on Christmas morning and he was already lighting up his second joint of the day. His voice was thick and slow and when Jody asked him if he was taking his meds, William said that if he wanted a lecture he'd call his mother. When Jody first moved to Victoria, she thought the distance wouldn't matter. Now she knows. Distance always matters.

Jody looks across the pond, pops the last of her sandwich into her mouth and rinses her fingers in the slimy water. Sometimes she has an overwhelming urge to pitch herself forward off the dock and disappear under the lattice pattern of the lily pads. Instead, she lies down and puts her hand over her face, inhaling the fresh, green smell of the lake. She should leave soon. The thought of work makes her stomach constrict and her neck tighten. She doesn't want to face Sal. The manager of the store works hard at being unpleasant, especially to her. And the customers, well, they're customers, impatient, demanding and too numerous. Her breath stops and gathers in her throat. Her mouth tastes like stale air. She reminds herself to breathe and pictures a white flower in her throat. Imagines herself swimming in that spacious white flower. The world is air.

She feels the light drizzle of rain on her face as she rises and jogs up the hill to her house. She can hear the phone ringing as she struggles to free her keys from the hole in her jacket pocket. When she opens the door, the ringing stops. She picks up the phone and an automated voice informs her she has one new message and one saved message. She listens to her saved message first.

Her friend, Katrina, sounds a little edgy with excitement and lack of sleep. "Hey, Jody. It's been a while, but I wanted to call to tell you we had our baby. Last week. A girl. Get a load of the name. Seraphina Jelena Papadopoulous Hart. Are we too cruel or what? We call her Stretch for short. She's so long and skinny, her legs just kind of dangle over my arms when I hold her. You know how short I am. I guess she must get it from her dad. Anyway, how are *you*? I should go now. Maybe I'll try again Sunday."

Jody replays the message again and leans into Katrina's happy voice. They have not known each other long. Not even a year. They were the only two students in a summer French immersion program who were over eighteen years old. At twenty-seven, Katrina wanted to take a brief vacation from her PhD. The immersion program was her idea of rest. At the same age, Jody had been contemplating a move to Montreal. An escape from Victoria, the deli and Sal. She decided to take advantage of the government-sponsored program that provided a place to live and a food allowance. The immersion program was also Jody's idea of rest.

After a few weeks, both Jody and Katrina complained of fatigue. They tried to go for walks to work off the extra weight they seemed to have gained for no apparent reason, yet they were too tired to do anything but marvel at their mutual listlessness. They blamed it on the humidity of Quebec's summers. At the final party, Jody drank one glass of wine and threw up. She'd thought it strange. She wasn't a puker.

Katrina returned to Toronto and Jody to Victoria. Two days back home and Jody realized she was pregnant. She refused to believe it, even when she peed on the little strip of paper and it turned from pastel pink to baby blue. She was overcome. She wasn't with child, child was with her. Frantic plans were made for the termination of the pregnancy. This was how both the staff at the clinic and Sal referred to the abortion. Jody disliked these careful words chosen to sterilize the event, take surgery away from flesh, take flesh away from flesh without anyone noticing. But words subtracted nothing from four weeks of weeping daily while waiting to have the procedure. And nothing could erase the days of bleeding baby out, the cramps, the large pads worn between her legs, which ironically reminded Jody of diapers. So ironic, she could weep again, except by that time, her eyes were cried dry.

Baby. When Jody talked to Katrina a few months after the abortion, she discovered her friend was also pregnant during the immersion program and had decided to keep the baby. Katrina described her round belly and they commiserated on their experience of morning sickness. For a month, it seemed like any odour could make Jody's stomach turn with nausea. It wasn't only pungent, bitter smells like garbage and gasoline that had this power. It was also fragrant, tasty scents like roasting chicken and perfume. Jody remembers throwing up in the shower because of her shampoo and being vaguely thankful for the warm water rushing over her because at least then she didn't have to make the extra effort to clean herself.

Katrina's message is coming to an end. "Anyway, how are *you*? I should go now. Maybe I'll try again Sunday." Jody saves it again and listens to her next message.

It takes her a moment to identify the voice. A woman, clearing her throat. "Hello? I hope I have the right place." William's mom. Jody stops breathing. Her fingers are cold as she rubs the hair standing on her arms. Mrs. Keller leaves her number and asks Jody to contact her as soon as possible. Her voice seems distant and uncertain. She clears her throat again. "Bye."

Jody doesn't bother to write down the number, she knows it by heart. She and William grew up together and his mother never moved from the old neighbourhood. Mrs. Keller was a stay-at-home mom who used to take Jody in after school and feed her granola bars until her own parents came home from work. William's mom seemed to be the only person who noticed Jody, which the young girl hardly appreciated since she took such pains to make herself as inconspicuous as possible, folding her skinny limbs close to her body, rounding her back, lowering her head.

With the phone tucked between her shoulder and her ear, Jody erases the message. She looks quickly at the clock and knows she'll be late for work, but dials William's number. She hangs up on his answering machine and tries his mother's. Mrs. Keller picks up on the first ring.

"Hello?" His mother always sounds like she's asking a question.

"Mrs. Keller. It's Jody Leski. I just got your message."

"Oh Jody? Dear, I'm so glad to hear from you. How are you?"

"I'm OK, Mrs. Keller. You?" Jody is watching the second-hand tick around the clock. If she's late for work the manager will do his best to make her shift hell.

"I'm fine, dear. Well, I'm not really fine. I'm . . . I'm not sure how to tell you this?"

"What is it, Mrs. Keller?" Jody asks, but already knows that something has happened to William. She chases the thought from her mind.

Mrs. Keller chases it back. "It's William, dear. He's in the hospital."

"Why?" Jody brings her finger to her mouth and chews at the skin around her nail.

"Well, maybe you know he hasn't been doing so good? I've been after him to take his medication. I don't like him smoking that stuff either, but the voices are worse when he stops taking the medication. The other day his boss phoned for me to pick him up from work. He was talking to himself. I went and got him, but you know William, he wouldn't stay here. He went home and the next day he was back at work."

William has worked at the same pizza parlor since high school. He used to give Jody free slices and, in exchange, she helped him cut mushrooms. Their childhood friendship continued, even though as teenagers it would have been easy for them to grow apart. In school, where the only thing that seemed to matter was looks, William was out of her league. He was tall, clear-skinned and blond.

She was tall.

The only thing that kept William from being really popular was his preference for comics over football and his habit of laughing at the most inopportune times. Jody still remembers the day their English class watched a BBC production of *Romeo and Juliet.* By the end of the play, all the girls' cheeks were damp with tears. William gave a big snort of laughter, which was incredibly loud because he'd been trying to hold it in throughout the whole tragic death scene.

Jody looked over at William's red face and knew exactly how he felt. She, too, had a long history of laughing at the wrong moments. Like when her mother got hit by that car. It wasn't serious, just a nudge, and Jody felt really bad, but she couldn't help herself. Even though her mother was now limping, the guy driving didn't know whether to stop or not because Jody was laughing so hard.

So she knew how William felt—laughing from nerves, not humour—and they stayed friends. Even now, Mrs. Keller's worried voice makes her shoulders tighten and her belly ache as a little unwanted giggle forms in her throat. She swallows it, making a loud gulping sound.

"Oh Jody, dear, are you all right?"

"Yes, Mrs. Keller. Please, I want to know what happened. Is William OK? Why's he in the hospital?

"I just don't know how to say this." Mrs. Keller's words become louder and no longer seem to have any question in them. "He cut himself, dear. He's cut himself badly."

Jody sinks to the ground. She plays with the end of her shoelace.

Mrs. Keller continues, "He was at work . . ."

"So, it was an accident?" Jody interrupts, wanting to believe that it's not as bad as she thinks, that it wasn't intentional.

"No. No, it wasn't an accident. It definitely wasn't an accident."

"But, Mrs. Keller, what did he do?"

"He cut himself. Not like the other times."

Jody tries for a big breath of air, but can't seem to get oxygen into her lungs. "Mrs. Keller, did William try slitting his wrists?"

"No, dear, no he didn't." Jody's lungs fill with air. "He didn't slit his wrists. He cut himself down below. Jody? Dear?"

Mrs. Keller's voice is once again filled with questions. "He cut himself down there. He says he heard voices. He says he listened to the voices. Jody? He tried to cut off his testicles."

Jody wraps the shoelace tightly around her finger, stopping the flow of the blood. She watches the tip turn pink, then white. She feels a giggle tickling her tongue. She gulps and gulps. "Mrs. Keller. I'm so sorry. I'm sorry. I have to go."

"I understand, dear. Call me when you can."

"OK." She hangs up. Her ear is burning. The giggle escapes. It's a quiet sound, like a small animal. Jody unties her finger and feels blood pumping under her skin. She rubs her eyes hard, pushing them back in their sockets. The softness of her lashes rolls against her skin. She fingers the phone cord and reaches down to carefully disconnect it from the wall. With her hands calmly resting on her trembling knees, Jody notices the red, raw skin around her fingernail.

The clock ticks away seconds. She grabs her apron and carefully locks the door behind her. Her right arm pumps back and forth as she walks. It feels like it's the only reason she can move forward. Her left arm hangs at her side—inefficient, useless.

She did not sleep well last night. She dreamt she was swimming. The water turned to fire. She couldn't breathe the fire. Jody knows that if she told this to her doctor, he would relate it to her panic attacks. The connection is too obvious. She thinks there is something more to this dream and tucks it away in a safe place. She will hide it from the doctor like she used to hide jujubes from William. If she feels generous, she might share later.

When Jody enters the deli, she sees Sal behind the counter and the manager, Mr. Grimald, standing beside him. "You're late." Grimald looks into her eyes and then slowly lets his gaze trail down her body.

Sal is constantly on Jody's back about the manager. "Just tell him off," says Sal. "Just say fuck you and the horse you rode in on." Jody is incapable of uttering such phrases. She can think them, but she can never speak them.

Jody gives Grimald no reason to think he can touch her. When the old man is near, she stands with her arms folded, her legs crossed and her eyes heavy with reproach. She has read articles about body language. She knows that even if people aren't aware of the body as a form of communication, they subconsciously understand the language. Jody concludes that Grimald has no subconscious.

Quickly donning her apron, she ducks behind the counter to punch in at the time clock. She can see Grimald from the corner of her eye, moving in. *Go away.* He slides behind her and pretends to need a pen on the shelf above her head. *Go away.* Even though there is plenty of room, he presses close. *Go away.* Jody feels an ungentle hand grasp possessively at her waist. He can't believe that she doesn't want him, but knows there is no reason why she would. This makes him mean.

"Go away," Sal says in a deep voice, which cracks on the last syllable. Grimald and Jody both turn to look at him, surprised. Sal directs his look at Jody. "Move, girl, can't you see you're in his way." Jody darts from the old man's heat.

Grimald stares at Sal and then Jody. "Don't forget to clean the bottom of the garbage," he says. "You guys left it over the weekend and now there's fucking maggots in the bottom."

Jody didn't work on the weekend, but she moves to the back where the garbage is kept. She feels triumph in Grimald's stare and pity in Sal's as they watch her pass. Later, smelling like sour meat and Javex, Jody returns to the front of the deli. Grimald is gone and Sal barely speaks to her.

He is punishing her because she won't sleep with him anymore. A couple days after the abortion, Jody went to his place, sat on the edge of his bed, woke him up and told him that she thought it was best if they stopped seeing each other. She didn't even have the energy for the whole it's-not-you-it's-me spiel. She just sat on his bed and said, "No more sex." He rolled over and said that it was OK. Jody went away satisfied, even a little happy, thinking the whole thing had passed rather easily. Apparently she was more to him than just a fuck buddy, though, because since then Sal has intermittently treated her to cold silences and long rants. She hears his silence and his words in the same way—indifferently.

Her four-hour shift at the deli passes neither quickly nor slowly. Sal has decided to talk to her again. He suggests drinks after work, but Jody doesn't want to go with him. It would be too easy to tumble beer-drowsy into bed, and then an hour later she would feel sick with her weakness and would have to tell Sal again how she thinks they should not sleep together. Jody would sleep with him, but she has no patience for his considerate approaches. Soft stroking hands, foot massages, wet mouth sucking at her toes, tender stares. He used to warm her side of the bed with his heat while she brushed her teeth. He has too much concern when all she desires is to be rag-dolled around Sal's apartment with beer bloating her belly and blurring her mind.

William has always had something to say about Jody's casual sexual relationships. He says Jody has low self-esteem. Jody has a problem with commitment. Jody has a self-destructive nature. Jody doesn't agree. She just likes the way men feel in the palm of her hand. Rough, smooth, solid, soft.

William and Jody kissed once. It was a long time ago. It felt incestuous. Jack Daniels forced their lips together and after, they laughed at the whole thing like it was a tragic scene from Shakespeare or a car accident. They decided they should always be friends and never lovers.

Jody is trying hard not to think about William, but images flash through her mind. She sees William closing the door to the pizza ovens. Moving through the kitchen to the counter where all the cooking utensils are kept in large, organized drawers. Opening the compartment marked *Knives* and choosing the sharpest, straightest edge he can find. William, casually propelled to the washroom by voices. Voices in his perfect, beautiful blond head. The smell of plumbing masked by cheap rose-scented air freshener. Voices.

She is too tired to be seen. Everyone's glance seems to

bruise her skin. She escapes into the walk-in freezer at the back of the deli, where she shoves her hands in her pockets and fingers her jackknife like prayer beads. The action calms her. With the chilled air stinging her bare arms, she systematically goes through the stock of chickens. She cuts pieces from them. They are not random pieces. She is collecting the joints at the ends of the drumsticks where the foot has been severed from the leg. They are smooth round bones with an iridescent quality. She will keep them in a sack and carry them around with her like marbles, a symbol of her sympathy for William.

Jody leaves work rolling the bones in her hand. Empty thoughts carry her home. When Jody opens the door, she is grateful. It is quiet, but the house seems busy, like an empty room just after people have left it. The silence is artificial and the air is unsettled. Jody's neck tightens. Her breath stops and gathers in her throat. She looks at the phone and plugs it in without really wanting to. Of course, it rings. She knew it would.

She picks up the phone and waits.

"Hello?" William's words are slurred. "Jody?" It sounds like he's just waking up. "You there?"

"Yeah, I'm here," Jody answers softly. She's aware she's lowered her voice as if trying to coax a bird to her hand. She clears her throat and tries for a normal, everyday tone. Just two friends chatting. "I talked to your mom."

"Yeah, she told me."

"How are you?"

"I'm doing OK. They got me pretty sedated. It's kind of hard to think."

"That's probably a good thing." Jody punches herself hard on the leg, wishing she could take back her words, find the perfect thing to say.

William gives a slow laugh. "I'm sure you're right."

Jody raises her fingers to her mouth and begins to chew on the skin at their tips. "How long do you have to stay in the hospital?"

"They're not sure. They're moving me to psych tomorrow."

Jody doesn't want to press William, but she also doesn't want to seem like she's avoiding the topic. "Do you want to talk about it?"

"I don't really know. I'm a little mixed up right now. I don't really feel anything. They say I'm still in shock."

"I can believe it." She punches herself again, hard.

William laughs again. "Anyway, I just wanted to call . . ." His voice trails off sleepily.

"I'm glad you did. You know you can any time. Maybe I'll try to come for a visit."

"That'd be good." It's taking him longer to reply, he's drifting. "I'm gonna go now."

"OK, William. Please . . ." But he's already gone. Jody lets her hands fall into her lap. A small drop of blood smears against her white apron. At first she thinks it's from the deli, but then notices how each of her fingers has been gnawed open by her teeth. To hide the damage, she folds her hands into loose fists and slides the phone into its receiver with her elbows. It begins to ring. She lets it, but it is too insistent. Her house becomes noise. She picks it up but depresses the receiver button without answering. Quickly, she dials the number to the deli and when Sal answers she freezes.

"Hello? Anybody? Is anybody there?" Jody can hear the meat slicer purring softly in the background. Sal breathes noisily. Jody pictures his lips slightly parted, cracked with small blisters. "Fire burns," he used to say and puff up his chest in self-mockery. His teeth are slightly discoloured, the enamel eroded by kerosene. Jody admired how he could turn breath into a blaze. She liked to watch him perform. When he blew fire from his mouth, the orange flames would shoot high across the dark sky with a soft roar.

"It's me," she says.

"Oh, hey. What's up?"

"I thought maybe we could meet later." She gulps air like water. He takes too long to answer. "What's wrong?" she asks.

"Maybe not," Sal says hesitantly.

"Why?"

"I kind of made plans already."

"Oh." She waits for him to say he'll change his plans. He doesn't. "Oh," she repeats. "OK, I guess I'll see you tomorrow then."

"Yeah, tomorrow."

"OK, bye."

"Sorry."

She hangs up. There is not enough air in the world. She has to leave her house.

The screen door bangs. Bang, banging behind her back as Jody jumps on her bike and coasts downhill towards the little man-made lake. No one is on the dock. The clouds and light rain have kept her neighbours inside. Gathering speed on her bicycle, she rides onto the pier with an ungraceful *thunk*. The wood is uneven and she feels her bike shaking under her. The motion makes her teeth chatter. She leans into the bike and feels her fingers burn with the pressure of her weight. She approaches the edge of the pier, rides to the end—and off.

She pitches forward slightly. The water hits her like a fist. When she comes up, she hears the startled loons complaining to the sky as they fly away. Her bike sinks and she turns over in the stale water to float on her back. The scum on the surface parts and outlines her body like a dense, dark halo. Water rolls off her cheeks. If she were crying, she might not even notice.

Jody thinks how easy it would be never to return home. Instead, she would go to Calgary and sit by William's bed. He'd tell her not to worry, assuring her that he's no crazier than she is. They'd both laugh. A laugh not from nerves. A laugh that would open their mouths and shake their bellies. Then she would continue east to see Seraphina Jelena Papadopoulous Hart, and when she held the baby girl in her arms, Seraphina's incredibly long legs would fit comfortably in her arms and look perfect against her height.

Resting in the water, Jody sees a small plane overhead. The sound of its motor is muffled to her submerged ears, but as the plane comes nearer she can feel the water tremble. She smells burning wood, takes a deep, full breath of air and lets her throat relax. Jody closes her eyes and pictures how empty her home is. The ringing of the phone sounds hollow. In the kitchen, she sees small, smooth objects tossed across the table. They are a sharp white against the deep mahogany wood. They are bones scattered in confusion with no one around to interpret their predictions.

Two Feet in Texas

The most generous thing said about Pina Delmorie in the twelve years she worked for the audio-visual department at the university was, "At least she doesn't smell bad." For the most part she went completely unnoticed, tucked away in the back room, making copies of departmental videos and transferring student films to VHS cassettes. While her co-workers in the adjoining offices clung to their windows like starfish stuck to the sides of an aquarium, Pina was content to sit in her dim chamber, the light of the TV monitor tickling her face and illuminating the squint that permanently furrowed her heavy brow.

Pina loved her job. If she wasn't watching a film, she felt like she was living in one—one of the worst kinds, an over-acted, self-conscious performance that amused no one, least of all herself. So she preferred staring at the TV screen, escaping into other people's drama. The only chore Pina did not like about her work was her rare interaction with the amateur filmmakers. Sometimes, if a job was late or the students were early, they would be sent back to her station where, much to her obvious annoyance, they'd incessantly ring the service bell and then lean heavily on the counter of the room's single small window. She resented this orifice with all her heart because it never let her fully relax, it never let her forget the outside world.

Recently, she'd been having an especially difficult time due to one student who made a point of always coming early. His name was Barker Gerber and Pina would cringe when she'd see his order on the "In" shelf. He seemed to have a talent for knowing exactly when she'd be in the middle of his film. He'd snake his long skinny arm through the window to open the door that was always kept locked in order to avoid just this kind of intrusion. After he gained entrance to her private sanctum, he'd stand behind her and provide a running commentary of his movie. "Oh yeah, this is the scene where we had trouble with the lighting, but I came up with the idea of pinning a red sheet over the window in order to give it that sexy, ominous look." Whenever he talked about his work, his middle finger would move restlessly over his left eyebrow—stroking, petting, caressing.

Pina would purse her lips, shift her bulk forward in her seat and focus on the screen, which invariably showed the same shaky, out-of-focus images of unskilled actors experiencing some kind of angst in poorly lit, badly painted student apartments or gloomy streets covered in brown slushy snow. Since the deadline for student projects was the spring, their films were always shot during the bleakest winter months of January and February and, therefore, all contained the same desolate backgrounds.

Today, she decided to confront her problem head-on and pushed his job to the front even though there was a rush order of departmental videos that was absolutely supposed to be done by noon. She quickly located his order, pried the metal film can open with her stubby fingers and expertly aligned the "Start" frame into position. She adjusted the sound reels, checked the exposure and colour and then let it roll, making sure that at the end of the *three two one* countdown, a beep cheerfully sounded in sync. Only then would Pina reach to the corner of her desk and pick up a pack of "Bee" playing cards. This brand was her favourite because of the small, child-like Joker dancing on the back of a large bee with furry legs and bulging eyes. With deft hands, she casually shuffled the deck over and over again, never dealing a game, never pausing in her habitual, meditative manipulation of the cards. Pina's usual frown of concentration seemed to ease slightly as she permitted herself to lean back in her chair and congratulate herself on avoiding one Mr. Barker Gerber.

"It looks like we're just in time." Barker's arm shot through the window. He popped open the door and Pina swiveled in her chair to fully face her enemy for the first time (usually she kept her back to him so as not to encourage their interaction). He towered over her from his impressive height of 6'4", came dressed in the battle gear of worn leather pants, which displayed a prominent bulge at the crotch, and was flanked by two flunkies whom she also recognized from the film studies program. Words of reproach dried up in Pina's mouth, and she exhaled a bitter sigh as she turned again to face the screen and curse his name.

"Watch this scene. It's brilliant." Barker waved a bony finger at the monitor. "We shot this from the top floor of the library building. Look at the people scurrying around like ants while in the background we see what's really important, what represents the present moment. You know what I'm saying? The Now." Pina could feel the boys behind her strain forward, trying to glimpse the crucial image. Squinting hard, she could just barely make out a young man masturbating. He was shot in profile and was staring intently at a wall painted with a mural of an enormous, fluffy, white-as-snow sheep. Pina thought the man was Barker himself, but it was hard to be certain since most of his head was hidden by a huge horned helmet.

"It's supposed to be out of focus," Barker asserted in defence of an unspoken criticism. "That's the point," he exclaimed. Pina could feel his followers nodding while they murmured their appreciation. "Yeah, cool, man." "Yeah, that's the point."

The final scene was a slow-motion shot of clouds gliding across a flaming sky. "A pretty image," Pina silently conceded. "As cliché as a gay hairdresser, but pretty."

"Great, isn't it?" Barker turned to his friends and leaned his ass on the back of her chair. Pina lurched forward to avoid contact and felt the zipper on her pants give way as her rolling stomach strained against the fastener. She looked down at the exposed pouch of pale flesh. In the cold light of the TV, her skin looked like blueberry Jell-O, the pockets of cellulite shimmering an even deeper shade. A line of dark, bristly hair trailed from her belly button to the waistband of her shiny white nylon underwear. Hastily, she folded her arms across her body.

Luckily, the boys hadn't noticed. Barker babbled on, "The people as ants metaphor has been done before, but I think my take on it, as a contrast to the physical pleasure we deny ourselves every day or feel guilty about or are *made* to feel guilty about, puts a whole new slant on it." His middle finger moved to stroke his brow.

"Yeah," Flunkie Number One, a short guy with dyed orange hair and a pierced brow, agreed. "And the music is phat, you know, it's all that." He shot his arm out in front of him and dipped his hand in the air, two fingers pointing down, mock rapper style.

Flunkie Number Two piped in, "That loft space is great. Like the whole space of it really says something about what you're trying to say." He was as tall as Barker but had muscles built on muscles. Cigarettes were folded into the sleeve of his tight black T-shirt, which had the brand name "stoopid" emblazoned across the front.

And still Barker babbled on, "I think it's really crucial we make a statement about society and how the expectations, no, *delusions* of the previous generation have contributed to our inability to really accept ourselves as we just live and breathe, man. As we just live and breathe."

Pina let out a derisive snort, which she immediately regretted when the boys' attention shifted in her direction.

"I'm sorry?" Barker said.

"You should be," Pina thought, but just shook her head.

"No, I'd like to know what you think." For a moment, Pina believed he sounded sincere, but she caught sight of his reflection in the monitor as he conspiratorially jabbed his friend in the ribs.

She lowered her gaze. She stroked the cards still clutched in one hand, their sharp, precise edges held strong against the anxious pressure of her thumb. She didn't want to answer. She didn't want to be their joke. She didn't want to be trapped here, hiding her belly, wondering exactly what capacity of sweat her underarm shields were guaranteed to absorb. She just wanted them to leave. Better yet, disappear in a cloud of smoke. Therefore, her surprise equaled, if not surpassed, that of the boys when she finally answered, "You're just bluffing, but you're not doing a very good job of it."

"Pardon me?" Barker's words were polite, but his voice held a challenge. Pina shook her head, dismal. Why had she opened her stupid mouth? She should let it drop now, but then she heard Barker's snicker, a contemptuous sound, and she found herself saying, a bit more loudly than necessary, "You're bluffing."

She hazarded a glance at Barker's reflection. The lines on the TV distorted his image. His skin quivered in the impatient light, but the weight of his stare hit the back of her head like the well-placed blow of a sledgehammer. His look said, "Just you wait."

◖◗

As Pina walked the last block to Barker Gerber's downtown apartment, she was filled with a profound regret. She regretted that her pants had split open, therefore making her feel more vulnerable and causing her to respond to a situation that she normally would have ignored. She lamented the confrontation that followed, which now seemed a surreal impossibility. Barker had replied with something like, "What do you know about bluffing?" His gaze drifted to the cards she fiercely held in her fist. And from there, with some goading from his friends, who seemed to thoroughly enjoy the exchange, she was invited to the boys' weekly poker game. A proposition thrown down like a glove.

Pina also mourned her acceptance of this duel and the closer she came to Barker's apartment, the more she regretted the very day her mother spread her legs for her father, the day she was born, the day after her birth, when her mother left her husband and newborn baby, and the day her father sat her down to teach her how to gamble.

Her father hadn't ever been a high stakes gambler. In fact, his relatively safe method of playing the percentages could hardly be called gambling at all. But he did manage to supplement his monthly welfare checks by picking up a game or two each week. As a child, Pina was a regular sight in the back rooms of the few bars on the strip that hosted the poker games. Her father would make her an omelette for dinner, wash the greasy eggs from her face and hands, tuck her favourite stuffed bunny into her arms and bustle her off to the games, which usually started to pick up after the supper hour. Pina would sit in a corner and gather the candy the other players always brought her. Striped, sticky treats that tinted her mouth red, purple, green.

Most of the men were labourers whose play was regular, if not consistent. One night, Johnny would go home smiling with a couple hundred in his pocket, the next he'd be counting his pennies to make sure he still had enough for cigarettes on the way home, while Bobby or Phil or Rusty gleefully fingered his winnings. Her father was the only invariable. He always came away on top, but never in a big way—thirty, forty, fifty dollars maximum.

Besides the local players, the games also drew a kind of travelling gambler. Even though most of the men knew they'd lose to the stranger, they welcomed the challenge and excitement involved in sitting down with a "professional." Pina's father only joined these games as the dealer, preferring to keep his money close to him. "No thrill in losin'," he'd tell Pina, giving her a friendly noogie. She'd smile as his knuckle grazed the top of her head, but she always admired the other men. To her young eyes there was a kind of nobility in their daring, even if they left the table shaking their heads in despair.

And she loved to watch the professionals, who came in a variety of shapes, sizes and styles, but all had the same slow sweep of hand as they gathered the pot and unhurriedly stacked their winnings into piles of coloured chips, looking so much like Lego castles to Pina's young eyes.

Pina, like her father and the men of her youth, was a five

card stud player, a game that demands bluffing skills since four of the five cards are dealt face up. Everything rests on the final card and whether you can make your opponent believe you drew a pair or you have a king in the hole that will beat the queen he has showing.

Out of all the films Pina liked to escape into, *The Cincinnati Kid,* starring Steve McQueen as The Kid and Edward G. Robinson as The Man, was her favourite. In the movie, the game is always five card stud. The Kid, a young, optimistic gambler, believes he can beat The Man and many rounds of poker ensue. During one game, a player, having just revealed the jack as his hole card, which loses to The Man's queen high, angrily demands, "How in the hell did you know I didn't have the king or the ace?" As The Man casually rakes in his winnings, he replies, "Son, all you paid was the looking price, the lessons are extra."

"The old bastard," Pina mumbled as she climbed the outside stairs to Barker's apartment, half cursing The Man for taking down The Kid, half cursing her father for dealing her her first game of poker. Standing at the front door, Pina could see through the window into Barker's brightly lit apartment. The two other boys were already sitting at a table pulled into the centre of the living room. They were sipping whiskey and laughing at something that Pina could only imagine was at her expense. When Barker entered the room, he too was smiling, and for a moment his gaunt face seemed almost soft. The whole scene looked like a stage setting. She could be walking into a movie, a high drama like the old westerns. When she entered the room, her boots would sound hard on the dusty, wooden floor of the saloon and she'd have a thirst for hooch and a craving for a game of chance.

Pina held her breath and rang the bell. Barker opened the door and looked at her with all the surprise of someone who's just found a mewling baby on his doorstep. His head backlit, his expression once again looked remote and cruel.

"Welcome to my home, Pina," he said, waving her in with

a dramatic flourish. "You've met Max and Alex." The boys at the table both nodded, leaving Pina to wonder who was who while she shrugged her coat off her stiff shoulders. "Sit, sit." Barker threw her coat onto a fake leather love seat and guided her to the table. Pina could feel Barker's long skeleton fingers on her elbow. They stuck into her flesh, which jiggled and rolled and bounced on her frame as she walked. She felt pierced by the boys' stares. She lifted her head, ignored the boys and took in her surroundings. The room was painted a deep red, the furniture was all black and chrome, and movie posters decorated the otherwise bare walls.

Pina scanned the images. Dressed in sleek, 80s black, David Bowie and Catherine Deneuve were depicted as proud vampires in *The Hunger*. Dreaded Cenobite Pinhead from *Hellraiser* presented the mysterious Chinese puzzle box as an offering, with the tag line "Demon to some. Angel to others." Suddenly Pina's eyes stopped. She gulped. Steve McQueen, holding a smoldering cigarette in one hand and a fist full of cash in the other, stared down at her. The Cincinnati Kid, here in Barker's apartment. Pina knew it was ridiculous, but she felt possessive, like a child grasping onto a favourite toy that someone was trying to tug away. The image was so familiar. The Kid looking sideways at The Man (not shown except for a hand with a big cigar). Ann-Margaret draped over one of his shoulders while Tuesday Weld looks on from behind. Bold print across the top of the poster exclaimed, *He'd take on anyone, at anything, anytime.*

Pina felt Barker's stare. He was smiling when she looked at him. "Can I get you anything? Beer? Whiskey?" he said pleasantly.

"Just some water please." Pina cleared her throat, patted her chest and sat at the table.

Barker returned, picked up the cards and expertly shuffled them while he explained the house rules. "Dealer calls the game, we have no limit, if you're winning you have to call a round before you leave, your hand is what you call—not what you have, and, as I mentioned when I invited you, the buy-in is twenty bucks." Barker placed a book in front of Pina and opened the cover to reveal a hollowed-out space containing three twenties. She reached two fingers into the pocket of her snug jeans and pulled out a crumpled, slightly damp bill, which she tossed into the fake book. Barker snapped the cover shut, pushed a stack of chips towards Pina and flipped a card in front of each player to determine who'd start the dealing. Barker's ace beat Pina's jack, so he gathered the cards and named the game. Pina could tell that he thought this was a good sign, that he still played a superstitious game of poker, preferring to believe in good and bad luck rather than simple chance. Hidden by her bulky sweater, Pina deftly undid the top button of her jeans, leaned back in her chair and settled into the game.

Her strategy was to play a conservative game while she got the feel of the table. Barker, like herself, mostly called five card stud when it was his turn to deal. The other boys invented outrageous games with lots of wild cards. In one game, everything was wild but tens and fives. They called it Spare Change. Pina anted up for these hands, but quickly folded. No use throwing good money after bad, as her father used to say.

As they played, the boys kept up a steady stream of chatter, mostly talking about movies. "An actor has to have range," Barker said. "Like Willem Dafoe, a white hat in *Platoon*, a black hat in *Wild at Heart*."

The boy with the muscles on muscles said, "I've always found him to be an attractive man."

"Really, dude?" the orange-hair boy questioned. "See, I've wrestled with that myself. But he was awesome as Jesus in *The Last Temptation of Christ*."

"My nemesis," Barker growled and inexplicably winked at Pina, who felt her face burn. Movies were the one thing that Pina could converse about, but she didn't know what to make of these guys. She decided to concentrate on the cards. She'd just won two small pots in a row and was warming up. Both the boys had already lost their initial twenty dollars and had bought in for more. Barker had a nice stack in front of him. He caught her looking at his chips and winked again, this time a private exchange, a flash of an eye so dark it reflected nothing back but shadow.

❦

Before this night, Pina had never actually played anyone other than her father. He stopped bringing her to the games when she was twelve, afraid that the newly developed breasts poking against her small T-shirts would prove to be too much temptation for one of the passing poker players. Everyone, including Pina, knew it was the act of an over-protective father since, even then, the homely girl, nubby breasts and all, did not have the power to arouse even the randiest man. Her body had already begun to spread into an indistinct shape, her heavy brows reached for each other over sunken, sullen eyes, her adolescent skin flamed with clusters of red, raw acne, and the flesh of her wide bottom quivered when she moved.

Pina was happy to stay home, fewer eyes to follow her, rest on her with pity, never with interest. She was most content curled into the safe arms of an over-stuffed chair, comforted by the distracting sights and sounds of television. Sometimes, her father still sat her down to games of five card stud. They would gamble with wooden matchsticks or toothpicks. By the time she was fifteen, she'd started winning, but retired soon after when she noticed a slight tremble in her father's usually steady hands as they flipped over card after card. When she was twenty she came out of retirement to entertain her father as he slowly died of cancer in a semi-private hospital room that depleted the meagre amount of money he'd been able to stash away over the years. Her father had been a bricklayer, but when Pina was born and his wife left him, he quit his job to look after the new baby. As she grew older, he'd mention looking for work, getting off welfare, but by this time his labourer muscles had wasted, and he didn't leave the house except for groceries and poker night.

By the time her father grew ill, Pina'd already started

working at the university, a job that adequately provided for her small needs, but left nothing over at the end of a pay period. In the hospital, her father had suggested she go to the games to earn a little extra. Pina had experienced an elusive feeling—pride. It was an isolated occurrence. Her father died the next day and Pina never played again.

Until tonight.

The cards felt good in her hands—their solid edges fit her palm like an old friend's handshake. As she shuffled, her eyes surveyed the table. They'd been playing for over three hours and she and Barker were about even, but she knew enough to realize that this could change at any point in the game. The boys had proven to be adequate players. Nothing like her father, but they could hold their own. Whiskey was on her side, though. The boys drank steadily, the hard liquor bringing a flush to their cheeks and a drawl to their voices—except Barker. He drank as much as the others and chain-smoked furiously, but his eyes remained sharp, his skin stayed a cool shade of white. He'd won the last two rounds. Pina needed something to change her luck. "One-eyed jacks and the man with the axe are wild. Two draws of two," she called. While she preferred the straight poker games, she had a good feeling about this one and, unlike her father who played by numbers and percentages, she tried to play by instinct.

Pina dealt the hand, looked at her cards and sure enough there he was, the king of diamonds, the only man to wield an axe in place of a sword. His hair curled down, his beard curled up and his usually stolid expression seemed almost cheerful to Pina as she regarded the pair of ladies accompanying him. In pure cinematic style, Pina imagined the king giving her an encouraging smile.

By the final betting round, Barker had drawn one card, the others had folded and Pina was looking at a third queen, which made four with the wild card. She glanced at Barker, who seemed pleased. "How many did you draw?" Pina asked, even though she knew it was one.

"One," he responded, closing his cards into a neat pile, which he placed in front of him. He seemed so smug, but Pina rationalized the odds of them both having four of a kind were slim.

"It's your bet," Pina reminded Barker, who was playing with his chips, dropping them onto the table with an annoying certainty that made Pina want to beat him badly.

"Check."

Pina knew he was fishing to see just how powerful she thought her hand was. Now, she could bet high, but that might scare him off. She chose to try to draw him in, "Three dollars." She threw the chips into the pot. Barker smiled.

"Three, and I raise you five." The other boys *aaahhed*.

"I see you and raise you . . ." Pina said, pausing. The boy with the dyed hair's exuberant shout of "You go, girl!" faded from his lips as Pina shot a silencing look in his direction. She picked up five green chips. "Ten dollars more."

When Barker didn't even hesitate, Pina had one moment of doubt. "What you got?" Barker now held his cards close to his chest.

Pina discouraged the smile that tried to cross her lips as she laid her hand down. "Four queens."

Again the boys chorused their appreciation, but Pina wasn't paying any attention to them as she focused on Barker's cards being laid in front of her one by one. Barker's deep voice growled out his hand, "Two, three, four, five, six, seven—of spades. Straight flush beats four of a kind any day, my friend." For one instant his cold hand covered hers in a clammy clasp of victory before it moved to rake in the pot.

Pina sipped her water and kept her expression blank as she berated herself for being too sure. She looked at the clock, a wrought iron design that looked vaguely animal-like, perhaps due to the small claw that ticked the seconds away or the manner in which it seemed to crouch on four legs at the edge of the table. "I'm calling a round," she declared. She could see no reason to stay. She'd lost all desire to fight and craved only her easy chair and TV. She felt like McQueen at the end of *The Cincinnati Kid*—whipped.

She passed the cards to the boy on the right, who called the game, four-four-four.

"Two-thirds of the devil," Pina joked, trying to muster some energy for the last rounds. The boys shyly laughed, obviously not sure whether to take her seriously. Barker also laughed—but only when he won again.

Next they played a seven-card game where all the cards are dealt down and are not looked at. "Blind stud," Pina exclaimed, nodding as they explained the game to her. "I like blind stud," she said agreeably, smiling until she heard Barker mutter, "I bet you would." The boys smirked. Pina's stomach constricted and she fixed her teeth together in a determined grimace.

Barker flipped all his cards to show a high straight. He tossed a green chip in the pot. "That's worth two dollars." He put his hands behind his head and sighed. Pina noticed two wet spots the size of quarters staining his armpits and was acutely aware of her own sweat running in neat lines down the small of her back.

She started revealing her cards, which first looked like a possible four of a kind as three sixes followed one after the other. She ignored their jokes about "the number of the beast" and "you'd better be careful." Focusing all her attention on the cards, she turned them quickly, willing another six. No other six came and she'd been so intent on the four of a kind that she almost folded on her flush to the ace. At the last moment, she declared her hand and bet big. In the end, no one could beat her and Pina stretched her short, thick arms across the table. It felt nice to pull in the chips and slowly stack them at her side.

Barker noticed her pleased expression and said with a mocking glint in his eye, "Maybe you want to stay a little longer?"

Pina stared him down—she knew when to leave. "No, this is the last game. What's it going to be?

"Five card stud."

Pina's heart gave a little squeeze of joy.

"Twice." Barker added after a pause. The boys groaned and all joy left Pina's heart as she contemplated the idea of Two Feet in Texas, which meant that any chosen game had to be won by the same player two times. This game could on forever and change people's fortunes because the pot kept building until one lucky player took it all. It was a game of pure luck since there was no point in bluffing until the very end when only players having already won one round were left.

"And since it's our last game, let's make it interesting." Barker's sly voice drew Pina's attention back to the table and she prayed he didn't do something stupid like add wild cards to the game. He shuffled the cards deftly. The low hanging light drew dark shadows in his narrow, handsome face.

"Well?" One of the boys squirmed impatiently in his seat.

Barker cocked an eyebrow. "Well," he began, "I propose that we up the stakes a bit."

Pina relaxed into her chair. At this point, what did she care if she lost everything? The fleeting glimpse of pride that made her accept this invitation in the first place had long ago crawled back into its deep comfortable hole. If playing this game would get her home that much quicker, so be it. "Whatever you want, Gerber. Deal the cards."

"Not so fast, little lady." His voice oozed sarcasm. Pina felt like pinching him hard. "I propose . . ." Barker stopped shuffling. The apartment became quiet except for the refrigerator working in the background, its motor snorting and chuffing like an old dragon. Barker slowly met everyone's gaze, his eyes resting on Pina last. "I propose we play for our souls."

The fridge cut out. The room grew weightily silent, an empty church where nothing moves except candlelight stirred by a draft.

Pina was the first to laugh. And, as the boys joined in and she hugged her sides in glee, she thought she had never before truly laughed. Barker remained still, watching the three with a slanted grin on his face, half patronizing, half enduring.

Pina panted herself to some semblance of calm and managed to gasp, "And how do you *propose* we do that." As the boys settled down into an uncomfortable hush, Pina noticed her heart thumped forcibly, tapping at her ribs.

"Oh, it's easy," Barker responded quickly. "We just write our full names on paper, they all go into the pot and whoever wins, wins everyone else's soul."

"And then what? We have to do your laundry, take out your garbage?" Pina suddenly realized she was speaking as if Barker had already won.

He smiled, "Nothing like that." He shuffled once more and offered the deck to the boy on his right, who cut the cards. "No, it's just the pure satisfaction of knowing I have your souls."

"This is ridiculous."

"Is it?" he replied archly. "But that's the game. Are you in?"

Pina waved her hand in his direction. She ignored her heart. Tap, tap. Just a movie, Paul Newman in *The Sting*, working the cards with fast fingers to reveal the ace of spades with each new cut of the deck. "Whatever, let's get this over with." She straightened her spine.

Barker looked at the boys. One shrugged, the other gulped his whiskey, they all were given pens and small rectangular pieces of paper neatly torn on the sides. Pina pinned the paper to the table with her thick fingers and scratched her name on the scrap. The black ink of the fountain pen smudged on the page, but the writing clearly read *Pina Maria Delmorie*.

"I thought Pina stood for something."

"Sometimes for Josephine, but I'm just Pina."

Barker looked at his name proudly. "Gerber is an old Swiss-German name from the verb *gerben,* which describes a process of removing the flesh from the skin of dead animals." He placed his name in the centre of the table and put a white chip on top of it. "Ante up," he said cheerfully.

Pina narrowed her eyes. She stopped herself from pointing out that Gerber was also the name of baby food, strained carrots, soft peas, mushed bananas. Food to gum, food for the toothless.

"Are you in?" Barker's voice brought her back.

"I'm in." Pina placed her name by Barker's and gently laid a chip across it. She wasn't sure how a name scratched on scrap paper could look so exposed. The boys followed and everyone seemed to inhale at the same time as Barker dealt the cards. When he won the first hand, everyone exhaled. Barker's hands flew around the table seemingly independent from the rest of his body. "Bats," Pina thought.

One by one the games were played out, each person breathing a sigh of relief when they won a hand. In the middle of the table, the coloured chips mounted. The players bet high because it was the last game. But Pina also knew they were reckless because of the names that lay under the pot. Finally, it was down to the last hand. "Everybody has one foot in Texas," Barker announced needlessly. All knew full well they had an equal chance at the riches.

Barker dealt the first hole card, which Pina restrained herself from looking at until the first up card was also dealt. "Ace high bets," Barker said, looking at Pina, who was aware of her strong start. Five card stud with no wild cards and no draws can often be won by a pair or even a high card.

"Ace bets three dollars," she said.

Everyone stayed in for the next card. Pina received a queen. "Possible straight," announced Barker. "Possible flush," he said to the next player. "King, two, nothing much going on there and a possible flush for the dealer. Ace still bets."

"Another three dollars." The boys groaned, but by this time no one would fold because everyone had already put so much money in the pot. By the next round of betting, though, both boys were out, leaving Pina and Barker to face each other. Barker's flush was looking good with three hearts showing. And it seemed like Pina was going for an ace high straight. If they both drew their card, Barker's flush would beat Pina's hand. The betting had gone up to ten dollars last round. The pot looked enormous. Pina started to try to estimate how much there was and then stopped, picturing only the four small pieces of paper under the pile, smothered by the chips.

Barker slowly flipped up the last cards. Pina was now showing ace, queen, jack, ten. She fingered her hole card and looked at it again. Barker also pulled a ten—of hearts—looking to all the world like a flush. He didn't even glance at his hole card. In fact, he put a chip over it and relaxed into his chair. "Ace high bets." Pina peered into his face. At this point, she didn't need to add more money to the pot and was curious to see what Barker would do. "Check," she said. Barker reached into his back pocket and pulled out two twenty-dollar bills. The boys were leaning so close over the table Pina could feel their hot breath on her arms when they exhaled.

"I don't have that much with me."

"I know you're good for it."

Pina couldn't read him and had a flash that she should walk away right now, save her forty dollars for a binge in the supermarket to try to forget this miserable night. But her soul? That little piece of paper with her name inscribed on it. How could she leave that in Barker's hands? She couldn't fold, even when she peeked at her hole card, which disappointingly revealed a two. The best hand she could make was ace high. If he didn't have the flush, that was enough, unless he had a pair under there. She studied Barker again. His middle finger wandered to his left eyebrow, stroking, petting, caressing, and suddenly she knew—this was his tell. Everyone has a tell, a nervous twitch, an uncontrollable action that surfaces only in a bluff. In the movie *Rounders*, John Malkovitch plays a Russian whose tell is the habit of splitting open Oreos. When his tell is learned, he shouts, "Meester son ov a beetch! Dat ees eet!" He hurls his cookies against the wall. "Nyet. Nyet. No more. No. Not tonight!" Pina knew if you learn a player's tell, you control the game.

"Yeah, okay, I'm in."

"Fuck!" The word exploded from Barker's mouth. "Fuck, fuck, fuck. How'd you know my flush was busted?"

The line from *Cincinnati Kid* ran across her mind—"Son, all you paid was the looking price, the lessons are extra." But Pina kept quiet, flipped her hole card and called her hand, "Ace high."

"Wait a minute." Barker leaned excitedly into the game. "You don't have your straight?" He flipped over his hole card and said, "Ace high, too." Hope lit his face and the boys were muttering "No way" and "Wow."

But Pina tapped her queen and said, "Sorry, boys. My kicker beats his." Then it seemed everyone let out a collective breath and Pina felt her muscles go slack. She sank deep into her chair. So tired, even her hair hurt.

They wrapped up the game quickly, everyone eager to part company. Pina cashed in just over two hundred dollars. With the chips cleared away, the four white souls lay revealed in the centre of the table, folded and crumpled. The names, scrawled in ink, showed through the thin paper. Pina thought about leaving them—it was just garbage after all. But then she felt the stab of Barker's stare. She forced her gaze up to meet his eyes, black holes that seemed to pull Pina in. Black holes that threatened to let nothing escape.

Slowly Pina reached across the table and gathered the souls.

Barker looked away. The other two boys studied the ground.

Pina dressed hastily and Barker closed the door behind her without a word, his face a dark silhouette indistinguishable from the assembly of shadows in the gloomy hall.

Outside, the cold air splashed against Pina's flushed skin. She walked with her head down and saw a dead bird on the sidewalk in front of her. When she arrived at it, she realized it was only a dried black banana. When she looked back, it had disappeared. Pina raised her head to the sky. She allowed herself a smile, which first twitched at the corners of her mouth and then grew large as she shoved her hand into her pocket and fingered four small scraps of paper that felt nothing like souls, but instead were warm and damp like the softest skin.

Cold Sleep

Caroline is awake and immediately aware that she does not want to be. She shifts under covers and pulls the sheet up around the back of her head to blindfold her eyes, leaving her nose and mouth free to breathe the cool air of the room. She can't sleep with something over her mouth; doesn't like the smothering hot air, air that she has breathed before, damp, thick, prison air. Even when she goes down on her husband, David, she pushes the covers to the bottom of the bed, ignoring his complaints of cold until, as she works her mouth, wet, sliding, swirling up and down, his objections fall silent.

Caroline can hear him moving in the kitchen as he tries to get his breakfast together without disturbing her. Sometimes she wishes he would stop being so quiet and solicitous, stop tip-toeing around her in distant, hesitant circles. She wishes he would fling the bedroom door open, bang his coffee cup against the brass rails of the bed's headboard and throw great handfuls of snow in her face. The dusty snow would take an instant to melt against her sleepy skin, but then its wet cold would soak into her dry thoughts and she would be truly awake for the first time in months. As she hears the front door close carefully behind her husband, Caroline curls her legs up close to her chest, tucks the quilt between her knees and pushes herself back down into that soft secret place of sleep.

When Caroline awakes a second time, it is pitch black and she hears a banging sound that she can't quite place, but sends her heart to her throat. Her eyes open wide with a sharp intake of breath.

She has no idea what time it is. The twenty-four-hour dark days of the far north in December leave her without the usual compass of day and night. It's quiet now. She's no longer sure there was a noise and strains to hear something, anything in the pall of silence that covers the house. If she were back home in Edmonton there would be some comforting sound to reassure her that she was not alone in the world; the splash of cars passing by her window on rainy days, the double honk of fire trucks moving slowly through traffic, the dull electric voices of her neighbour's television through the thin walls of her old apartment.

Here, nothing.

She throws the covers off her hot body and slips her feet into David's thick plaid slippers. The sound came from the front of the house, but she's still cautious as she looks out the bedroom window. All she sees is her own face reflected in the glass against the darkness outside. Her hair is tangled and fuzzy on top. David asked her if she wanted him to wash it for her last night. She was confused at first, imagining removing her hair like a fur rug and handing it to David to put in the machine. When she understood what he meant, she just smiled vaguely, shook her head and thought, *why?*

In the distance, Caroline sees a snowmobile, its headlight shining round and small, as the machine moves across the tundra from the town in the direction of the airstrip. The store must have ordered supplies from Inuvik. When Caroline first came to Sachs Harbour, these were the days she most looked forward to, the arrival of fresh food. A long-time vegetarian, Caroline preferred a salad to any other meal. "Where do you want to graze tonight?" David would tease her when they were dating.

In Sachs Harbour good produce was scarce. "We're going to get scurvy," Caroline joked when they first moved.

David replied seriously, "You can get vitamin C from eating meat."

"A lot of good that'll do me," Caroline mumbled.

"What?"

"Nothing."

David had applied for a transfer before they were married. He hadn't mentioned it when he proposed over dinner at her favourite Italian restaurant, Chianti's. She went there for the salad, crisp dark lettuce, finely chopped onions, black olives and flowers of green pepper tossed in a black pepper vinaigrette that Caroline tried and tried to reproduce at home, but to no avail. When she asked the owner for the recipe, he avoided answering her. "But then we wouldn't see you anymore, Lina." And while she smiled politely, she felt a sharp stab of anger with the realization that he would never tell her.

The owner left the table. David shifted in his chair. She felt his toe nudge her ankle, like that of a demanding child trying to get attention. She pulled her leg away. David cleared his throat. "Will you marry me?" he blurted out.

A fine line of sweat dotted his hairline and his face glowed red against his pale blond hair. Caroline could now feel his long legs shaking under the table in a frantic, rhythmic twitch.

"Yes," she said, but with no conviction. She seldom made a decision without sleeping on it, but as she looked at David slumped happily in his chair, she had the feeling there was no other option at the moment. As Caroline returned his smile, a piece of cracked pepper that was lodged between her teeth scraped against her lips.

After dinner, David stood at the door to her apartment and said shyly, "I was thinking that maybe we should stop sleeping with each other until after the wedding." Caroline chewed at her lower lip. Their sex life was her best tool to measure how things were going between them. So far it'd been good. David gave a caress like a compliment.

Now he stood with his hands shoved in his pockets, waiting. "Sure," Caroline conceded. As he gave her a light kiss goodnight, she realized her lower lip was still clenched between her teeth.

Alone in her apartment, Caroline decided she'd better call home. Her father answered. "Caroline!" he said, and she realized that he already knew. David was a friend of both her father and brother from the RCMP, and everyone in her family had been aware of the proposal before he made it.

Caroline slept deeply that night, dreaming of a desert. She

stood alone in the dry, barren land and was frightened until she saw a soft face in the glow of the round moon. She lay on the ground and moved her arms and legs. When she stood again, she looked down to see the angel she had engraved in the sand.

◖◗

Caroline has stopped dreaming. David tells her that of course she still has dreams, she just can't remember them right now. Caroline has always remembered her dreams, she uses them as road maps, following their thin black lines across her waking day. In the north, her dreams started to slip away with the disappearance of the sun. As the days got shorter, she had less energy and slept longer, but it was a dull slumber, no images played across her mind. When she drifted off, she felt like she'd fallen into a well, a hole so deep that there was not even a glimpse of light from the top, that opening to the other world where people moved and laughed and ached and loved.

As she watches the snowmobile vanish behind a hill, Caroline feels her eyelids droop. Should get dressed, she thinks, make a coffee, try to be awake when David comes home, but the lure of the warm bed is too strong. She turns her back to the window.

Suddenly, she hears the sound again. A hesitant knock at the front door, tapped out in the familiar rhythm of a friendly song, ending with a sharper *tok tok*. Caroline freezes. Her mind goes blank. The sound, so recognizable, seems strange, the beat of a drum in a fairy-tale land. She looks around her dim room for answers. The bed lurks in one corner, piled high with covers, a small hole denoting the space Caroline recently vacated. David's extra uniform hangs on the back of the door. Through the window, ice glows darkly, the polished shine of onyx. She knows where she is. If someone asked her, she'd readily reply, "Sachs Harbour." But she can no longer remember exactly *how* she came to be here and feels vaguely disoriented, a dizziness that comes from turning circles too fast.

When David had announced his plan to go north, Caroline agreed it was an opportunity. It seemed both practical, what with the large salary he was offered, and an adventure. She was tired of working twelve-hour shifts at the hospital. Even while studying to be a lab tech, she had known she wouldn't last long. She'd entered the program out of high school after taking a career placement test provided by the counseling department. The results had suggested pastry chef or laboratory technician. Since her parents wanted her to go to university, the first option was quickly dismissed.

After four years, Caroline discovered that she liked seeing blood magnified under microscopes, a community of cellular action, but she hated collecting blood from the patients. Her days and nights filled with endless rounds of pressing flesh and more flesh to find veins, easing in cool metal needles and holding tubes of thick liquid still warm against her hand.

Caroline knew nothing of Sachs Harbour when she agreed to the move. After she said yes, the RCMP arranged a meeting with another wife who had lived in the north a few years ago. She met the woman in the cafeteria of the west end station and drank instant cappuccinos dispensed from a machine into plastic cups.

"I don't know what Sachs Harbour is like, but Inuvik wasn't so bad," the woman said. "Next to Yellowknife, it's the largest community in the northwest, so there was always fresh food and activity in the town even when the days became shorter and darker." Caroline nodded politely and watched the skin of the woman's neck fold over itself in long horizontal creases, wobbling slightly when the woman laughed. And the woman laughed a lot, talking on and on about how the people up north were real funny and had the fattest babies and at least there wasn't much danger for the Mounties, breaking up the odd fight or so when the natives were pissed, but mostly just standing in as figureheads.

Caroline carefully read the pamphlet the RCMP had given her to prepare her for the trip and discovered that many of the communities were dry, in an attempt to control a widespread problem of alcoholism. The brochure also cautioned that the term "Eskimo" was a name the natives resented because it came from the white explorers and meant "meat-eater." Caroline closed the pamphlet and imagined herself debarking the plane and greeting the Inuit community with smiles and kisses and all the right language that would convey her open-mindedness and acceptance of their culture. When David and Caroline arrived in Sachs Harbour, the narrow gravel landing strip was empty except for a few boys running beside the plane throwing handfuls of dirt into the propellers.

She and David had been flown from Edmonton on a Hercules C-130 transport plane that belonged to the Canadian army. It was bringing a communications truck to Sachs Harbour so the RCMP had arranged the lift with the army, and Caroline found herself sitting in the back of a flying warehouse for six hours. She was strapped into a foldable seat made of netting with the truck only a few inches from her knees. David moved around a lot, talking to the army guys and going up into the cockpit. Caroline didn't want to be a nuisance, so she remained seated, staring into the side of the tall box of the green army truck with her matching beige and burgundy luggage set lined up by her feet.

Caroline had always been slightly claustrophobic. Stepping onto an elevator, she would have to remind herself that the trip was short, that she would be off in no time, that there was no reason to panic. She had always preferred to be on top when she and David made love. She found the missionary position fine as long as they were moving and panting and grinding and loving, but when they came and David collapsed heavily on her chest and legs, pinning her to the bed, she found it difficult to control the urge to squirm out from underneath him as quickly as possible.

When David strapped her into the seat on the transport plane she immediately started going through a breathing technique she had learned from a book about yoga she bought at a garage sale. On the cover, a slim woman sat cross-legged in a red body suit and white leotards. Her smile stretched across her face like a toothpaste ad. Caroline and David had laughed at the woman's dated feathered hairdo, but it was not long before Caroline could recite the description of every breathing exercise in the book. She would see the words against her closed eyelids as she forced herself to take in air. And let go.

The Cleansing Breath: purifies the bloodstream. Inhale deeply. Whack your abdomen in forcefully to expel air. The sensation should be one of having been punched in the stomach.

⟪ ☾ ⟫

Caroline pushes air from her lungs as she hears the knock again, this time a sharp rap. She drops to the floor. The bedroom is at the back end of the house, but her instinct is to get down, out of view of the window. Her heart beats fast. She's cold, but her forehead is slick with sweat as she crawls to the bedroom door, breathing hard.

She has been here for four months and not once has someone just dropped by. Since winter hit full force, she has only seen David. His comings and goings are quiet and regular as if intentionally lulling her to sleep. The knock comes again and then Caroline remembers.

Last night, when David returned home, he crawled into bed and tried to wake her. He shook her gently. She groaned. He shook her again and started to talk. An army plane had arrived, carrying some people to work with the communications truck they had brought to the Harbour this summer. One of the troops was a woman. Caroline tried to focus, still caught in the depths of what could have been a dream. Yes, she was having her first dream in months when he had shaken her. She strained to avoid his voice and focus on the images in her mind.

David's voice kept crumbling the dream. He thought it would be good for her to talk to someone new. He'd invited the woman to the house. He was sure the woman was nice enough and that she would be able to fill Caroline in on what was happening at home. Wouldn't Caroline like to know what was happening at home? Caroline could recognize the concern in his voice, but she was too far from him, too close to the dream. That was when he offered to wash her hair.

She agreed to the visit to satisfy him, to silence him before the dream escaped her entirely. She was standing at an intersection. The corner of 109th Street and Jasper Avenue. The hospital where she was born was down that road. During high school, she had worked in Albert's Restaurant across the street from the hospital, pouring cup after cup of coffee for nurses who, after three hours of continuous refills, would leave her a thirty cent tip among the cigarette ashes they had spilled onto the table. The wind was beginning to blow, raising dust from the dry street. Sand stung her eyes and skin. She raised her head to the sky, trying to breathe clean air, and saw a black, moonless void. She fought to move away.

David was now snoring softly. Caroline eased out of bed and went to look out the kitchen window, still half asleep. At home, in the summer, the trees grew large and, crossing any bridge in the city, there was a perfect view of the lush green river valley. Here, where the dry tundra stretched across the island and into the ocean, there were no trees.

Caroline didn't stay up for long. She moved back to the bedroom, climbed under the covers and stared at David's large back. His breath was steady and heavy. She remembered lying awake nights in Edmonton after they made love, watching his face, wondering if she would see him grow old. Now she could not stay awake long enough to contemplate the new lines easing themselves into the skin around his mouth and eyes. Now, when David touched her, she shrank from the contact, folding into herself, unable to imagine the kind of effort it would require to open her arms wide and embrace another body. She preferred instead to curl up by his side and work the saliva in her mouth, bringing wetness to her dry lips. She would then take him into her mouth and, as he moved against her tongue, she would try to focus and concentrate. She would empty her mind and, above all else, she would try to ignore the overwhelming urge she had to bite down.

With the chalky taste of the dream still in her mouth, Caroline lay in bed and felt her teeth press together. Her jaw was clenched so tightly, she knew that when she awoke and tried to eat a banana, her whole mouth would ache. Her eyes itched and burned. She squeezed them shut and almost touched David's warm shoulder before she floated, drifted and sank.

◖◗

This morning when she woke to hear David in the kitchen, Caroline had not remembered the conversation or the dream. Now, as the knocking persists at her front door, she cannot evade the dream or the noise. She knows she is unable to face the smiles of a stranger brought to her from that far away home.

The room suddenly seems small and airless. Her eyes search the dark corners for options. She doesn't want to hide and keep still. The walls press in and she thinks, *Escape*.

Caroline opens the bedroom door and squirms along the floor, careful to keep David's floppy slippers on her feet. She will need them.

The living room is in shadows, one small plug-in nightlight glows against the baseboards. Caroline can just barely make out the dark shapes of furniture. When they first arrived, Caroline was impressed by the new home provided for them by the Mounties. The front door opened onto a large room that included the kitchen and living room. An island in the kitchen served to make more counter space and separate the two spaces. In the living room, a floral print couch and chairs circled a huge TV set. Two fat glass lamps sat on side tables by each chair and a matching wooden coffee table rested in front of the couch.

As Caroline had looked around, she felt something familiar tug at her memory and then she recalled that she'd admired the exact same room in the Sears Spring catalogue. Even the layout was the same. The only thing that was different was the size of the television—theirs was definitely bigger. The bathroom was next to the one closet in the house and was approximately the same size. For the first week, every time David went to wash his hands in the sink, his broad shoulders would scrape against the wall of the shower stall and he would burn his forehead on the low hanging light bulb. He would curse, she would laugh, they would kiss.

In the days following her arrival, Caroline discovered that most of the houses in the hamlet were furnished the same way. When David told her they were going to visit the mayor's house, she had fixed her hair and put on a light cotton dress that had a top like a sailor's suit and was David's favourite. She wore her navy blue pumps to match. It was, after all, only a short walk. Outside, she could hear the gentle sound of waves and, as they mounted the small hill that separated their house from the main part of town, the ocean came into view.

It was a cloudy day, the water looked flat and grey, shimmering slightly as the waves crested close to the shore. At the foot of the hill lay a group of buildings that seemed to huddle together. Immediately, Caroline saw just how small Sachs Harbour was, maybe fifty houses arranged along a few hard-packed dirt roads. Certainly fewer than the five hundred residents proclaimed in her information pamphlet. When Caroline increased her pace to get a better look, she twisted her foot in a huge pothole. Only a few minutes later, they had reached the mayor's house, and her ankle was already swollen and throbbing over the rim of her shoe.

The mayor's house was like most of the buildings in the hamlet. Few windows broke up the straight lines of wooden siding, and it was raised on stilts to protect the structure from the constant shifting of the ground as it froze and melted and froze again. Bright red paint covered the mayor's house though, as opposed to the faded greys and browns that were peeling off the other houses. David carried Caroline up the stairs and didn't even have a chance to knock before a young boy opened the door. The child seemed to already know David. He smiled a big-cheeked greeting and led them through a boot room filled with shoes and coats scattered everywhere.

In the living room, Caroline was surprised to see a TV bigger than theirs blasting out a MuchMusic program with five kids watching a video, fully entranced. As David paused to greet everyone over the blare of the music, Caroline stared at the screen. A man with long, dark hair and heavy white make-up lurched in close to the camera, and Caroline could see the fine lines of his mouth cracking under his red lipstick. She could catch only fragments of the lyrics he was screaming. *The beautiful people, the beautiful people. Can't see the forest for the trees. Can't smell your own shit on your knees.* "Marilyn Manson," an older girl told Caroline. She had long dark hair and was wearing an intricately beaded vest designed with pictures of polar bears and the moon. When the girl spoke, Caroline saw a perfectly round silver stud piercing her tongue. A younger boy proudly informed Caroline that they were the first family to get over twenty channels. Now it seemed that every house had a satellite dish, clusters of large silver flowers stretching to touch the sky. As they left the front room, Caroline could just barely hear the girl's voice singing softly with the TV. *Hey you, what do you see? Something beautiful and something free.*

A woman called to them from the back of the house. They followed the voice and arrived in a cluttered kitchen. Clean dishes were stacked on the counter, shaggy musk ox skins were piled on a chair in the corner and baby toys were strewn across the ground. David went to the freezer for ice for Caroline's foot while Caroline sat on the edge of the chair indicated to her by the fast sweeping motion of the mayor's hand. The woman facing Caroline was young and attractive. She wore her dark thick hair plaited in the back, exposing high cheekbones in a soft, round face.

"That's a nasty sprain," she said, shaking her head over Caroline's foot. The baby in the carrier on her back gurgled.

"You're the mayor?" Caroline asked, realizing too late that her surprise might seem rude.

The woman laughed. "You can just call me Beverly," she said. "And you're not the first to have that reaction. At thirty-three, I was the youngest mayor to be elected and certainly the first female politician."

David placed a bag of ice on Caroline's ankle. She sucked in her breath, how could something so cold burn so much? It wasn't David's fault that she twisted her stupid ankle, but she was angry. She pushed these thoughts aside and tried to focus on what he was saying. "Beverly's family is one of the most respected in Sachs Harbour. Her father is the oldest ranger in the north." He looked at Caroline's blank expression. "Remember, I told you how rangers are volunteers who help the regular police force, acting as liaisons between the locals and us RCMP."

Caroline nodded, but felt defensive. Before the move, David had talked a bit about his new post, saying his job would be easy. In Inuvik, there were more problems. When the sun went away, people got restless, killing time by drinking. In the bars, the boys would buy beer and whiskey, but almost everyone also drank the white moonshine that was cheap and always available. David had explained that Sachs Harbour was a dry community so he wouldn't even be faced with the challenge of controlling bar fights.

She had paid attention when he talked, nodding her head encouragingly and even making notes, but it had all happened so fast, she couldn't be expected to remember everything.

David glanced at the clock. "In fact, I'm supposed to be down at the station now."

"You're leaving?" she asked.

"Duty calls." He pecked Caroline on the forehead and shook hands with the mayor.

"Some coffee?" Beverly asked after he left and Caroline nodded, trying hard not to feel abandoned.

"Yes, please," she said, suddenly craving the taste of something familiar.

Beverly turned out to be a much better resource for information than Caroline's RCMP pamphlet or David. Situated on Banks Island, Sachs Harbour was the most northerly community in the Northwest Territories and so small it technically couldn't even be called a town. "The hamlet has a history of plane crashes because the airstrip is so rough," Beverly said. "Only a few months ago, a small Cessna went down in the lake we used for water. Five people were killed, including three from Sachs Harbour."

The mayor paused. "My aunt was on the plane." Her eyes shone black and wet. She blinked quickly a few times, but when she continued her voice was strong. "In a community this size, everyone had a friend or relative who died that day. Something the government seems incapable of understanding."

Caroline shook her head, she wasn't following.

"Sorry, I'm going on," Beverly laughed. "My husband always says, 'Don't get her started.'"

"No, it's interesting. I just want to be sure I'm understanding it all." Caroline looked forward to dinner with David that evening because she would finally be able to tell him something about this strange place they had moved to.

Beverly took a deep breath and explained, "When the accident happened we asked for funding to build a five-kilometre road for the water truck to easily be able to access another lake. There's no way in hell we're going to drink from the lake our relatives drowned in. I don't see what's so hard to grasp about that. But the government just stalls."

As the mayor talked, she cleaned the carcass of a caribou, strewing meat and skin and bones across the table. Caroline sat with ice packed on her ankle, gulping down her culture shock with her coffee.

Finally, David returned to help her home.

"Why didn't you tell me the mayor was a woman?" Caroline asked, leaning into his arm as she limped across the tundra.

"I thought it'd be a nice surprise."

"I looked stupid." He brushed away her complaint with a wave of his hand.

Their small house was only a few steps away. Caroline balanced on one foot while he opened the door. He came back to collect her, grunting as he lifted her into his arms. He stumbled through the entrance and deposited her in a chair, saying, "I have to get back to the station."

She looked up. "Now?"

He knelt beside her chair. "It's my first post away from Edmonton, Caroline. I'm just trying to do a good job."

"I know," she said and took his hands. "I guess I'm just starting to understand what a big move this was."

David gave her fingers a squeeze. "I'll try to be back early."

The door slammed shut behind him and Caroline sat alone in her kitchen. Absentmindedly rubbing her hand where tiny spots of blood from the caribou had sprayed her, she tried to focus on her breathing. *Whoosh hiss whoosh hiss.*

The Cooling Breath: has a calming effect on the body. Form your tongue into a trough. Inhale air through this trough with a hissing sound. Exhale.

Whoosh hiss whoosh hiss.

☙ ❧

Caroline crawls along the floor. Pawing the air, she puts her hand out in front of her, followed by a slow knee, and then the other hand. The knocking comes again, louder this time and more insistent. Caroline hears her heart beating out time like a metronome. It seems like hours have passed, but Caroline knows it's only been minutes. Hidden behind the couch, she risks coming up to a crouch and peers into the kitchen. A silhouette darts in front of the window and puts a hand up to the glass to look in.

Caroline ducks. Her knee lands on the remote control. A light flickers and then the TV is on. A blur of colours kaleidoscopes across Caroline's squinting eyes. The cheerful sound of a girl's voice calls out, "One, two, that's right, keep your butt tucked in tight and push and push . . ." Caroline fumbles for the remote to find the off button.

Much of Caroline's first months were spent in front of the TV. Everyone told her it would be her friend and that when she was homesick she could watch programs to comfort her. But she didn't want to see warm beaches and women working out in bikinis. Aerobics in sunny climes did not remind her of home, only of a life more glamorous than hers. And, truthfully, the programs broadcast from Edmonton she did tune into did not ease her homesickness but intensified it. On ITV news, she could see glimpses of familiar scenes, the Silly Summer Parade on Whyte Avenue, the Folk Festival in Mayfield Park, a fire in the north end by her brother's house, an overview of the city showing them spraying for mosquitoes. Everything she saw made her feel disconnected, like she was a child staring into a city contained within a plastic globe filled with water and fake snow that would fall if she shook it.

Lately, Caroline does not watch TV when she's alone, preferring the silence to its constant background babble. When David is at home, the TV is always on. He eats his dinner in front of it, one hand on his fork, the other on the remote control. He changes channels quickly, his thumb deftly entering the numbers of his favourite stations. Sometimes he hands the remote to Caroline, who takes it because she feels she must. She slowly flicks through all the channels, including the weather station and Arts and Entertainment. She can never decide which program to choose, and at David's impatient urging to just pick anything, please, she begins to do her game of eeney-meeney-miney-moe. Melrose Place or a rerun of Seinfeld. *Eeney-meeney-miney-moe, catch a tiger by the toe, if he hollers let him go, my mother said to pick the very best one and you are not it.*

When Caroline first met David, he thought this process of elimination was funny. Now when she does it, he rolls his eyes in exasperation. He cannot believe, in the end, that this is the only way she can make a decision. Caroline often wonders what would have happened if another man had proposed to her at the same time as David. *Pick the very best one and you are not it.*

◖◗

Caroline points the remote at the TV. The scene of the beach shrinks to a point of light and then vanishes, but the person outside the door must have noticed. A female voice calls out, "Hello, anybody there?"

Why doesn't she leave, Caroline wonders and then clearly pictures David approaching the woman. He'd let a shy smile grace his lips, and he'd say, "My wife seems to be a bit down. It'd be a real help if you could swing by our house for a visit." The woman would nod sympathetically and promise to make sure she kept knocking. Caroline might be sleeping, David would warn, but it wouldn't be a bad thing if she were woken up.

Caroline still remembers having energy. It was August, when Caroline and David arrived in Sachs Harbour. The days were still long, the sun a small burning ball suspended high in the immense sky. They had missed the twenty-four-hour days and Caroline gratefully learned that they had also missed the summer bugs. Caroline had tried to keep busy, taking walks, sometimes with a dog or two from the hamlet trailing behind, keeping her company. At first, she stayed close to the town, making sure to keep some familiar landmark in sight. Slowly, she began to go further, her heart beating a bit more quickly as the view surrounding her lost all trace of the known. She was always a bit relieved when she decided it was time to turn around. In the evenings, she'd cook dinner and treat David to long massages. It was their honeymoon, after all.

And Caroline continued to visit the mayor. They would sometimes grocery shop together, Caroline helping Beverly home with her bags, even though the other women seemed to have no problem carrying enough food for her husband and five children while toting her youngest in a sling on her back. Caroline loved how all the babies were always being held by someone—mother, grandparent or one of the older children. "You can't spoil a baby," Beverly said, and Caroline suddenly remembered the daycare by her apartment in Edmonton where workers took the children for walks, stringing them together with plastic leashes and dressing them in orange high-visibility vests.

Sometimes Beverly would have time for a coffee in the restaurant attached to the Co-op, but usually Caroline went there alone. The room was small, sparsely furnished with plastic patio furniture, and was never empty. People sat in groups of three or four and all greeted Caroline with a friendly hello when she entered. She would bring a book with her and try to read, but would always end up staring blankly at the pages and eaves-dropping on conversations. At the coffee shop, she learned that John's new ski-doo had trouble with its starter, that Beverly's boy had to leave Sachs Harbour in September to continue his schooling in Inuvik at the age of thirteen and that the price of mandarin oranges at Christmas would be thirty dollars for a box of two dozen. As she listened, Caroline was always careful to turn the pages of her book regularly, even though she had not read one word.

Caroline also occasionally dropped in at the recreation centre to talk to the director, one of the few other people in the community who was not a native of the hamlet. Roy had lived in Sachs Harbour for eight years, ever since he'd first visited while working on a government census project.

He was a large man. When he smiled, which was often, his eyes disappeared in a tight squint and dimples materialized as two long grooves along his cheeks. It was difficult to imagine him as anything other than jolly, but he was the first to mention how hard life could be in the far north. "After spending my first winter here, it became clear why Bev was fighting to have the rec centre built. Even if you are working full-time, which a lot of people aren't, the endless night does a number on your head."

Caroline watched Roy as he spoke and was distracted by his

eyes, such a warm shade of brown. She nudged her chair a little closer and leaned forward.

Roy gave her a friendly smile and continued, "Doesn't matter if you were born and raised in the north, everyone gets bummed out. The rec centre gives people a place to go. You'll see, when it gets dark, there'll be people playing basketball at four in the morning. Everyone loses track of day and night. You have to find your own rhythm."

A chill ran along Caroline's spine. She leaned back with a sigh.

Caroline had started to dread the coming of the winter months. Even back home, she'd get depressed with the lack of sun. Last year, her doctor suggested taking St. John's Wort and weekly visits to a tanning salon. This year, she'd started taking her pills early. It was already dusk by late afternoon. The same as in Edmonton, really, Caroline tried to reassure herself. But here, the sun didn't rise until noon. "Why do you stay here?" she asked Roy one day. "I mean, the Inuit are amazing people, they're very warm and welcoming, but it's so cut off."

Roy shrugged, "I've felt more isolated in the middle of a big city. I was never so lonely as the times I took the subway home during rush hour."

Caroline nodded, but she didn't really understand. With her claustrophobic tendencies, she'd imagined that she would love the great empty space of the north, but she hadn't been prepared for how her voice was swallowed by the vast landscape, only to be offered back by the wind as an unknown sound that echoed in her own hollow shell.

Still, something drew her outside. Her walks had become longer and longer. She spent hours roaming the beach and marching across the tundra. On overcast days, the ground, water and sky all became the same shade of grey, and Caroline could imagine fading into this gossamer land, becoming so light even her footsteps disappeared.

Roy interrupted her thoughts. "Eskimo," he said. "You always say Inuit, but the people here refer to themselves as

Eskimo. They think of the Inuit as an entirely different people who live in the northeast."

Caroline was frustrated, couldn't she get anything right? When she went to the mayor to confirm this new bit of information, Beverly smiled and said that the term really meant *raw* meat eater and since she, herself, liked to chew the tender morsels of caribou right off the bone, she had no objections to the word. She grinned broadly and pointed to her mother sitting quietly in the corner of the kitchen. Deep lines creased every inch of the old woman's skin. Her face was a face that could only belong to the moon. She pulled back her lips in a toothless grin and showed Caroline the morsel of fish stuck between her gums. In the north, the elderly sucked on frozen raw Arctic char like sweet hard candy. Caroline smiled back, went home and threw out the RCMP pamphlet, deciding that she knew nothing of this place, except it was the end of October and it was already below freezing.

Caroline's retreat into sleep was a slow process. One day, she didn't go to the Co-op and instead sent David for groceries. After a week, when the mayor asked David about her, Caroline sent a message saying that she was fine, but didn't feel like visiting. It was very cold, after all. She preferred to stay at home snuggled into the couch, wrapped in the blue and pink afghan her mother had sent her. Feet tucked under her bum, she stared blank-eyed into the empty television screen and sipped coffee, trying to shake off the drowsiness that constantly enveloped her. The caffeine left her just as lethargic, but with a tense jaw. Still she tried.

On the couch, Caroline would shift with effort, moving her limbs slowly, thick heavy elephant legs. Lowering her head, she listened to the silence. She felt the blood pumping at the base of her throat. The coffee maker gurgled in the kitchen, brewing the second pot of the day. Her hair rubbed against the cushion as she sank deeper into the couch. Through half-closed eyes, Caroline could see the bulk of the TV lurking in the corner. And then she'd drift off. Gone into the place where she didn't think about anything, didn't miss her friends or family, didn't worry about how her husband spent more and more time at work even though he, himself, said there wasn't much to do there. David often admitted that his partner, a native of Inuvik, could run the show himself, yet he still used work as an excuse.

The last time she left the house it was two weeks ago, just before Christmas. David had called from the station to tell her it was the coldest day so far, -60 C with the wind chill factor.

She knew he was calling not to give her a weather report, but to check up on her. He was concerned that she didn't see anyone but him, couldn't understand why she didn't want to talk to her family, and was troubled that she was still in bed when he came home from work. One evening, he walked into the bedroom, flicked on the light and said, "It smells in here."

Caroline pulled the sheet down from around her head. "Like what?" she asked, absentmindedly sniffing the air.

"Warm," he said. "Like something animal." There was a warning in his voice. Caroline could hear it, but couldn't respond to it. Even though the lights were on all over the house, she could feel the dark outside, a black shroud as heavy and soft as velvet. That's where she wanted to be. That's where she was when she closed her eyes.

"Why don't you go over to the rec centre?" David prodded. He wasn't going to let her close her eyes. "Roy's been asking about you, says maybe you could help out there."

Caroline couldn't imagine being around all that activity; basketballs thudding against gym floors, people gathering for tea, the radio perpetually blaring out CBC programs, Roy laughing and joking with kids. She pulled the sheet over her head again. "Can you turn off the light?" she mumbled and David did, as he closed the bedroom door with just a bit more force than necessary.

On the -60 day Caroline decided to go outside. Maybe David was right, maybe she just needed to get out and see some people. She put on a layer of thermal underwear, two sweaters and David's extra ski-doo suit. She wore heavy boots, thick mittens and covered her head with a Balaclava. The frigid air stung her eyes and she moved slowly against the strong wind. Before reaching the town, she met a group of young boys who laughed at her bulky attire. Caroline liked the boys, even though they were often loud and too energetic. She preferred the girls, who would stand quietly beside her and sneak their small warm hands into hers. As the boys left, one of them pushed her. They ran off when Caroline fell, leaving her flat on her back, staring at the sky through two woolen peepholes. She struggled to get up, but the clothes restricted her movements. When she finally was able to rise to her feet, she was wet with sweat. She turned around and went directly home without buying the apples she'd been craving when she left her house.

She hasn't gone out since. Sometimes David threatens to carry her outside and throw her in a snow bank. He shakes her shoulders gently and says, "Caroline?" He keeps suggesting she return home for a visit, but it seems he, too, is paralyzed by her languor.

⟨◎ ◎⟩

Inching across the floor, Caroline realizes that she is finally completely awake. The heat of the house is smothering, the clamorous knocking too much noise. She craves the hush of wind across land and the space of sea and sky. At the small back door of the house, she grabs a parka that hangs on the wall and slips it on. With swift hands working at the lock, she wiggles the rusty latch until it gives way. The door opens silently. From outside, she hears a soft impatient curse from the woman visitor. Sweating from her sudden movements, the cold gently rubs against Caroline's exposed skin. She is still wearing her soft pink flannel nightgown, which the wind lifts, sliding its cool hand between Caroline's legs. She gathers the coat around her. It's not -60 anymore, but the wind is not gentle. Her hair moves, her eyes tear. She starts to walk and breathe.

The Complete Breath: increases resistance to colds. Breathe deeply, consciously. First, fill the lower part of the lungs. Then, fill the top of the lungs. Exhale slowly. Do not slump.

Dry snow circles her ankles in soft puffs. Her feet are still hot from being inside and she barely notices the sting of ice on skin. Even with the oversized slippers, Caroline quickly reaches the hill leading into the hamlet. She glances back at her small house and sees the figure of the woman walking away in the other direction towards the camp the army has made by the airstrip. She looks to the ocean, so close, but indistinguishable from the tundra except for its enormous flatness.

No one is outside. Moving through the town, Caroline smells the gas of a snowmobile that has recently been used. She sees people through their windows. The mayor, washing dishes, talks into a phone tucked efficiently between her ear and shoulder. Tom Apiana, a local carver, sits at his table surrounded by the horns of dead animals. His hands are idle, his eyes blank. Amos Nasogaluk, one of the few still living off the furs he collects from his trap line, lounges in front of his TV. He is surrounded by endless faces of children, all laughing at the same time, becoming still and then laughing again at some sitcom joke. Caroline imagines the sound of their laughter, wet, musical giggles that come easily, but as she moves towards the frozen ocean, all she can hear is the silence cut by the flapping of her gown. Only a few minutes have passed, but Caroline feels a lifetime has been spent in this dark. Her breath comes rapidly now, it scratches against her throat. Caroline reaches the beach and continues to walk out onto the ice, tasting the air with her tongue.

She knows that she can never walk far enough to escape the lights of the town, so she keeps her back to them. Standing straight, eyes wide open, she chooses to face the blank night. Caroline can finally feel the cold. It covers her completely. During this time of constant dark, the moon, too, disappears as though every vessel of light snubs the north. It is only when she makes a small turn back towards the town that she notices the dim stars, flickering like distant fireflies in the sky.

The Corner of Star Star

Tory sits on the curb in front of a gas pump and the general store. The pump, rusted with rounded top, sprouts from the ground like a lone mushroom. Beyond it sprawls an expanse of flat, open field. But across the road, Tory can see two other businesses and the few houses that comprise the small town. On one corner, an old two-storey hotel stands in disrepair. The top floor has collapsed into itself, yet the bar on the ground floor remains open with a sign in the window promising a *Cold Beverage Room*. On the other corner, directly across the street, sits a small stucco box. Tory can't quite see into its windows, the morning sun bounces off the glass and hits her eyes. A small black spot stains her vision as she looks away.

Past the buildings stretches more level landscape. Silent yellow fields reach to the immense sky. Tory shifts her gaze to a puddle and is surprised to find more sky, the still water perfectly mirroring a tiny portion of the blue above. Her hand drops to the ground and begins sifting through gravel, searching out the brightest rocks. She throws a coral-coloured pebble and then a larger stone the hue of sunflowers. The shallow pool ripples, turning the reflected sky into a circle of small waves. Thin clouds bend and sway in the water. Tory's eyes stray to her car, crookedly pulled off the road, looking lost in its dusty surroundings. Breathing a slow sigh, she closes her eyes and leans back.

Except for quick catnaps and pit stops for gas and fast food, this is the first time she's stopped since leaving her home three days ago. While on the road, she hasn't spoken to anyone aside from the usual pleasantries. "Nice enough for you?" cashiers ask across the land. Across the land, Tory replies, "Yes."

Tory's last full conversation was with her boss when she called to inform him that she quit and was leaving the city as soon as she hung up. This she did more quickly than expected, since Mr. Barnes seemed intent on nastily swearing at her once he realized that there was no changing her mind. When he called her a "drab cunt," she disengaged the phone from her ear and softly replaced it in the receiver. Outside the phone booth, commuters had just begun to file onto the freeway, jamming the lanes that led into Toronto. Tory didn't mind—she was headed the other way.

◖◗ ◖◗

When Tory opens her eyes, nothing has changed.

On the road, everything is still. No dust stirs on the horizon to tell of an approaching vehicle. The song of cicadas is constant, shifting in intensity and vibration, but always there, filling in what would otherwise be dead silence. Tory rises and crosses the road to the small square building. Pressing her nose to the window, she sees that it, unlike the rest of the dust-covered town, glows with cleanliness. The floor is checkered black and white and gleams with fresh polish. The shelves and glass display cases are empty. Three round tables stand in the centre of the room. Two white chairs are placed neatly at each table, their backs forming six perfect metal hearts. Above the cash register, a large sign in scrolling, cherry red print proudly proclaims *Stella Estrella*. Underneath, in smaller print, the words BAKED GOODS offer the only elucidation. Tory steps back from the window and sees a note on the door. The letters, first scribbled in pencil and later darkly outlined by a black felt marker, simply read *Closed*.

She imagines that this is the sign they will hang off her desk at General Life Insurance. *Closed*. But she knows this is unrealistic, that Mr. Barnes will have had a temp in her place by the end of the first coffee break. She knows that she will not be missed, except perhaps by Heidi, her one friend who also works at the insurance agency. But Heidi would understand Tory's flight. She would even applaud it. Heidi is all irreverence, a small woman who wears power suits and appears serious, but who always took the time to joke with Tory.

Heidi used to throw disparaging glances in Mr. Barnes' direction where he sat in his office with his feet up on his desk, his generous bulk teetering precariously on the back two legs of his chair. "Did you have to help him get his feet up?" Heidi whispered, her confidential tone making Tory feel just a little daring. Heidi's mocking email messages had the same effect. Tory always read them quickly with a knot in her belly, like when she was in grade school, passing notes during class. She made sure to delete this correspondence, but printed and saved a copy of her favourite, a photo of Mr. Barnes and two other managers in a clinch at the golf club. The three men were holding up the ten pounds of ribs they'd just won in the company's annual tournament. They were sweating and their noses were red from sunburn, excess scotch or both. Heidi had added sepia tones to make it look like an old western WANTED poster. At the top, she'd inscribed the words: *The Good, the Bad and the Ugly.* Mr. Barnes was in the middle. Tory suddenly realizes that she will miss Heidi.

She will not, however, miss work, her parents or the mice.

◖◗

Tory moves away from the bakery to stand on the corner of the town's main street. The general store seems to be open now. A woman and a boy enter. Tory feels her stomach growling for breakfast. She checks the road again, but all she sees is a dented STOP sign leaning in the muddy earth, the word *NO* spray-painted across it in black.

She smiles at the sign, noticing that the graffiti is old, the paint faded and cracked. In her father's town this kind of vandalism would be hastily cleaned up, especially on a city sign. Tory's father is the mayor of one of the numerous small communities on the fringe of Toronto. He also has a medical practice that Tory's mother helps run. Her father is a small man with large hands and a loud voice. Her mother is too skinny. When Tory talks with her mother, she notices that the blue veins around the older woman's eyes are the exact pale shade of her irises. When Tory listens to her father, she only notices the floor.

Tory knows that she has not made her parents particularly proud, but she hasn't caused them any trouble either. Her parents have never had to worry about her, never even had to give her a second thought, really.

Tory had worked as a clerk for General Life since she was eighteen and lived in the same apartment since she was twenty. This winter she turned thirty. Her routine remained much the same, work, TV in the evenings, Sunday supper with her parents, and an occasional outing with Heidi, but in the months leading up to her birthday, the numbers— 3 0 —loomed large in her mind. Three decades, zero experience, she thought and pictured herself trapped inside the 0, a hamster on a treadmill going round and round. Tory shook her head.

For weeks on TV, the CBC had been running the same Heritage Moment about the settlers of the prairies. The short sketch opened with a shot of chuck wagons bumping across a dry riverbed. The voiceover told the story of the Canadian government's plan to develop the vast expanse of savage country. Pioneers were lured from the east or far away countries with the promise of 160 acres. Free! In The Wondrous Land of Opportunity! *Go west,* they said and when Tory closed her eyes, she heard this call. A plan started to form.

On her birthday, she bought the Malibu station wagon. The month before she'd taken driving lessons without telling her parents. "Why would you want to do that?" was her mother's standard reply to anything she thought might add complications to her daughter's life and by extension her own. "Hassle," was another favourite response. All Tory's ideas—maybe taking music lessons, maybe getting a dog, maybe going south for a holiday—became a *Hassle* once mentioned to her parents.

So when Tory signed up at A-1 Drivers, she kept quiet. But when she bought the Malibu, she was so excited she had to tell someone. Heidi arrived at her place with two tall bottles of

Italian sparkling wine. "To celebrate," she said. They toasted each other often and drank until Heidi proclaimed, "I'm getting silly." Every once in a while, they would raise their glasses to the old station wagon parked outside, a long black beast squatting in the snow bank.

At the used car lot, Tory had sat in shiny, tin-can cars. Originally, she'd pictured herself in something compact, sporty even, but that changed when she spotted the Malibu. She liked the weight of the sturdy station wagon and reasoned that the long bench seats would be comfortable to sleep on even if the back of the car was filled with her stuff. The salesman said that the reduced-to-sell price "couldn't be beat" and Tory agreed, signing her cheque with flourish despite the nervous complaints of her stomach.

She hadn't yet told Heidi her plan, preferring to celebrate the reality of the new car rather than a vague, uncertain dream. After Heidi left, Tory passed out in front of the TV and didn't wake up until one o'clock the next day. The first thing she did as a thirty-year-old was to ease herself off the couch and look out the window at her car. Crystalline patterns of ice covered the glass, leaving only a small, clear rectangle that perfectly framed the Malibu still parked in the same spot, but no longer black. Brightly painted letters and little cartoon designs decorated the sides of the station wagon. "Heidi's had a busy morning," Tory thought fondly before running to the bathroom to throw up.

Her lingering hangover actually helped her manage supper with her parents. The headache numbed their words and her muscles were too tired to become tense. She smiled when she opened their first gift, a card with a Canada Savings Bond enclosed. She winced when they gave her their second present, a bright blue budgie in a shiny gold cage.

"The man at the store said they are extremely easy to keep," her mother said and handed her a stack of pamphlets explaining how to care for the new pet. Her mother's voice kept rising to compete with the increasing volume of the twittering of the bird. "Much easier than a dog," she shouted. "Food and water, of course. Every day. And clean the cage once a week. No fuss. No shedding. No *Hassle*," she screamed.

Tory kissed her parents goodnight and took the bird home on the bus. She did not tell them about her car.

❦

Tory takes another brief glance at the Malibu as she crosses the street to the general store. *Hometown Confectionery* is etched into the door and painted brown. The store also houses a restaurant that boasts *Largest and best steak in the west*. Reaching the door, she tugs at its heavy wood and glass weight. A bell chimes.

She is greeted by the stinging citrus smell of an orange peel freshly dug into. In the corner of the store, the small child she'd seen going into the store with his mother holds a huge fruit in his hands. The boy is dressed in cotton shorts and sneakers. His rounded, bare belly protrudes over his waistband. Juice runs down his arms and smears a clean path around his dirty mouth. His mother rushes over. "Joshua, I told you to wait till we got home," she fusses. "Now the car will get all sticky." She bustles the boy out the door past Tory, throwing a brief smile in her direction.

Their departure leaves only three other people in the store, two customers at the back and a man sitting behind the counter, newspaper spread in front of him. *Fact or Fiction? Truth or Tale?* demands a headline. The man scowls. His black eyebrows grow thickly together across his forehead, a startling contrast against his pale skin and white hair. A navy blue apron is tied snugly at his waist. He grunts a reply to Tory's request for "a coffee, please" and groans his way out of his chair, shuffling into the kitchen.

He reminds Tory of her landlord, another gruff old man who for years has hardly acknowledged her existence in his building. When she saw the first mouse, she didn't tell her landlord for two reasons: she had hoped the problem would just go away and she wasn't good at making demands.

Heidi had also influenced Tory, telling her friend about how she'd kept a mouse in one of her plants. She built a small ladder from Popsicle sticks to aid the tiny animal into its new home and named the mouse Sheila. Tory had imagined that she, too, could accommodate such a small, cute creature, but then one mouse became two became three became much too many. Soon, she was endlessly cleaning their shit from her bookcase and desk and cupboards. The only room they hadn't invaded was her bedroom. But even there, she could hear the mice moving in the walls as she tried to sleep, scratching and shifting and chewing and scurrying. The pillow held tightly against her head didn't help.

Still, she preferred to try to solve the problem herself.

The hardware store by her home was an organized place with polished faucets and glistening garden tools. In the *Pests* aisle, as she contemplated her choices—live traps, kill traps and poison—she became uncomfortably aware of her intent. "Premeditated murder," she thought as she decided on a box of blue pellets that promised to not only kill the mice, but also shrivel their corpses into tiny puffs of dust. *Irresistible bacon and cheese flavour*, the package claimed. *One feeding does it!* Her guilt grew as she distributed the poison around her home. The next morning she squirmed as she sat at the kitchen table and watched the mice brave daylight to feed at the deadly buffet.

❧ ❧

Tory shakes her head to dispel this image as she walks past shelves stocked with Campbell's soup and paper towels. The restaurant is at the back of the store. The seating consists of one wooden picnic table. Two people are already there. She hesitates, but the man at the counter waves at her to sit down. She slides in beside a small elderly woman with yellowed hair. The woman's shoulders curve inward under a pink cardigan, and her freckled hand darts quickly to the toast and jam on her plate. "Morning," she acknowledges Tory.

"How was your night?" questions the man sitting opposite them. His face is incredibly tanned and, though much younger than the woman, his skin is thickly textured with laugh lines and wrinkles. Around the collar of his T-shirt, which says *I like my beer cold and my women hot*, is the thinnest line of pale, vulnerable-looking flesh.

The two strangers address Tory with a familiarity that suggests nothing much gets missed in the small town. Tory shifts on the hard seat and settles into the small talk. "Quite the dump of rain you had here last night."

"Yeah, dammit, we'll be waiting another day for the wheat to dry out before we can bring it in. Last year, we didn't get started till October. And even then, I had to leave one field out."

"That's what you have? Wheat?"

"Nope, mostly it's canola now. Good thing, too, 'cause it's not so fussy whether it's dry or not. Canola. That's what everyone wants."

"Less cholesterol in canola oil," murmurs the woman. A few dry toast crumbs fall from her mouth.

"I heard that our cholesterol level is all controlled genetically," offers Tory, "and what we eat can only affect the levels minimally. So this whole cholesterol craze is just something else cooked up by food corporations to raise sales and give people something new to buy."

"Yep." The man nods his head, the bill of his baseball cap ducking up and down in agreement. "I like my steak," he adds. The three fall silent contemplating cholesterol.

At General Life Insurance, if clients' cholesterol was high, so were their premiums. Mr. Barnes had the idea to hold a Cholesterol Challenge. Drop your levels and win a day at the spa! No one entered. He also decided that letting employees wear jeans on Friday would increase morale, and he designed a polo shirt with *GLI Inc* written ever so discreetly across the left breast. He bullied the employees into purchasing the polo shirts and then, not even a month later, circulated a memo banning the tops, explaining that Jeans Day was cancelled since so much outside business was conducted on Fridays.

Tory used the shirt to wipe out the bottom of her budgie's cage. She still felt no affinity for the bird. The whole winter had passed, spring too, and she hadn't even named it. Then, one night, she discovered the reason her house was still infested by mice.

She'd been on the phone with her mother, who was calling to remind Tory about her yearly dental check-up. Even though Tory's dentist hadn't mailed anything to her parents' address in years, her mother still managed to know exactly when Tory should be getting her teeth examined. "Don't forget to tell them about the heart murmur," her mother said.

When Tory was twelve, her father found a problem with her heart. It was the weekend and he was showing her how to use his stethoscope—this, when he still thought she might follow in his "footprints," as he used to say, and Tory would picture his black work shoes, tops made of stiff leather shined to a high gloss, soles deceptively smooth, the corner of the heels sharp.

Her father moved the cold steel of the stethoscope across her slim back with the precision of a professional while instructing her to tell the patient to breathe in and breathe out. Suddenly he stopped, grew quiet and bowed his head to listen. The stethoscope stuck to her damp skin as he pulled it away. "Irregular," he pronounced and called one of his friends, a specialist, for a second opinion.

At the time, Tory was a fan of high romance and happily entertained the thought of herself as a frail young woman who suffered from the vapours, but was irresistible to all eligible suitors. This vision of romance soon disappeared as she listened to her parents talk.

They met in the living room. Her parents remained standing and spoke over her head, never catching her eye. Her father's voice droned on. It may be minor, just a sluggish valve that would cause no real problem except the sound of gurgle and slush. Or it could be more serious. In this case, precautions would have to be taken. Infection could be fatal. Strenuous exercise should be avoided and antibiotics always taken when going to the dentist to prevent germs from the mouth getting into the bloodstream.

My bloodstream, Tory thought and stared at her parents hard, willing them to look at her. "We'll just have to see," her mother said and spun on her heel to make coffee in the kitchen. Her father escaped to his study. Tory sat alone. If she remained very still, she thought she could hear the beat of her heart in the silence of the room.

The specialist saw Tory first thing Monday morning, a favour to her father. The ultrasound came back with the best news—no murmur of any kind had been detected. "I could have sworn," was all her father said about his mistake. The whole incident lasted all of three days, but Tory's mother wrote a note to the school excusing her daughter from gym class and still mentioned "the murmur" whenever Tory went to the dentist.

"Just tell them what your father heard," her mother was insisting, when Tory noticed the noise in the front room. Tory hadn't told her parents about the mouse problem—her mother had an intense fear of the little creatures, her father thought them "filthy"—so she didn't even pause in the conversation as she walked to the living room and flicked on the lamp. Usually, the mice scattered with bright light. This time nothing happened. The budgie made a small peep from its cage that sat on a stand in the corner of the room and was covered for the night. Tory heard another scratching sound and walked warily towards the cage, all the while keeping up a coherent stream of "yes, mom," "no, mom" and "I know, mom." As she reached the budgie, she could hear a rustling in the cage. She slowly stretched out a hand to give it a quick tap and two mice dropped to the ground.

She exhaled sharply.

"What?" her mother demanded.

Tory lifted the cover to the cage and four more mice hung from the material.

She sucked back her scream. These mice also tumbled to

the floor, knocking against Tory's legs as they fell. She couldn't catch her breath.

Her mother persisted, "What? What's happening?"

"Nothing, mom. Really. I just stubbed my toe. Gotta go now. Bye." She hung up, collapsed on the couch and nervously scanned the room for any sight of the mice. The budgie looked down at her and she suddenly realized that all this time the mice had been climbing up the cover to get into the cage. And they'd kept coming to her apartment, despite many of them dying from the poison, because they couldn't resist gorging themselves on birdseed. Tory looked up at the bird and felt awful. "You poor thing," she crooned and dipped her fingers in between the bars of the cage. The budgie bit her and Tory felt even more awful. That was the night she named her bird. Spike. The next day, Tory finally asked her landlord for help. He complained about the expense of an exterminator and reluctantly supplied her with a selection of traps—all the options Tory had first rejected at the hardware store.

That evening, she set traps with peanut butter and cheese as bait, keeping the sticky pads in reserve, not willing to risk the chance of finding a live mouse fixed fast in glue. "If large rodents are present traps may be taped or tacked to the floor," the package explained helpfully. Tory shuddered and decided that the time had come. She went to bed making plans.

There was enough money in her savings account. She could put most of her things into storage and Heidi would probably keep Spike for her. She wouldn't tell her parents until she was safely out of town. "When I'm well on my way," is what she said to herself as she drifted off. Overnight, she caught three mice. In the morning, she was surprised how peacefully she'd slept through the sound of the traps snapping throughout her apartment.

◖◗

A small shiver runs up Tory's spine as the old man plunks

down a cup and saucer in front of her, the coffee sloshing dangerously. The noise seems especially loud in the quiet, dusty air of the store.

Her "thanks" receives another grunt in reply. The pink cardigan woman starts to chew again. Feet shift under the table. Tory searches her mind for something to say and remembers the radio program she'd been listening to in the car last night. She shapes her mouth into a smile and points it in the woman's direction. "Did you hear about that scuba diver they found in the forest fire?"

"I don't think so, but I only pay attention to the local news."

"Well, apparently there was a huge forest fire in Montana somewhere. After the fire was out, a crew came to see what kind of damage had been done and they found a guy in the middle of the burned out woods. He was dead, but the weird thing was—he was dressed in full scuba gear."

"There's a guy a long way from home." The man leans back with his arms crossed.

"How'd that happen?" The woman leans forward over her plate.

"They figured the fire-fighting plane had scooped the guy up where he was diving in a nearby lake. Nobody realized what had happened, so the plane carried him out to the woods and dropped him with the water over the fire."

"Shit, that's no death I'd wish on anyone. What about that story, Fred?" the man calls over to the storeowner who slowly turns the page of his newspaper on the counter.

"Sounds to me like one of these urban myths," he declares without glancing up.

"It was on the radio," Tory says.

"Doesn't matter." The owner punctuates his remark with a rattle of the paper.

"You want a myth?" the man with the baseball cap pipes up. "Did you hear about the dinosaur bones they found down south of here?"

"That's no myth," the woman shakes her head at Tory. "It's

some story, though. That little town was almost as small as this one. Probably never had five hundred people drive through there in ten years and now it's got five hundred tourists traipsing through there every day."

"You know what the dinosaurs died of, don't you?" the man questions.

"No."

"Boredom." The man guffaws. Tory gives a polite chuckle. "Pretty soon we'll be the damned dinosaurs the way things are going round here," he predicts.

"Not much was moving out there last night."

The woman munches up her last piece of toast. "Hardly anyone left here but us old folks and we go to bed early. Habit, I suppose. Everyone else is broke and had to leave town, or going broke."

"That's why the town's called Banksend," yuks the man.

At the counter, the owner stands and disappears into the kitchen.

"Is that what happened at the bakery next door? The sign says closed, but it looks like it never opened."

The owner reappears with a pot. Tory gratefully accepts more coffee. It's so weak a dash of sugar makes it taste sweet as cotton candy. The woman covers the top of her cup with a steady hand. A crumpled, crooked, steady hand. The man rises and throws some change on the table. "That's it for me, got to get back to work to pay for all the damned coffee I drink here." As he reaches the door, it opens, ringing in another person. "He's for you," the man says to Tory.

"Hi," she greets the young guy who's just entered.

He, too, is suntanned, wears a short-sleeved plaid shirt and has curly red hair that stretches into incredibly long sideburns. He looks at her and then checks the sheet of paper he holds in his hands. "Tory?"

"I'll be right out."

When she'd left Toronto, there were so many things she couldn't picture happening to her. Tory used to spend hours at work mindlessly processing insurance policies while fantasizing about driving across the country to see the ocean. But her dreams were never detailed, they were elusive feelings of freedom and excitement. She certainly never imagined her old Malibu station wagon breaking down in the middle of the prairies and, if she had, she probably would have thought of it as an insurmountable problem, an overwhelming inconvenience. But reality was quite different.

It was dark when she first heard the clanking sounds in the front of the car under the passenger side. The Malibu started to lurch forward, then sputter. She turned the radio down just as the engine stalled. By this time she'd reached Banksend, so she coasted the wagon off the road by the gas pump. A quick look out the car's window and it was clear that the town was completely shut down for the night, even the hotel bar. She noted the phone booth outside the general store, pulled out her comforter, and immediately fell asleep with her head on the armrest and her knees tucked securely under the steering wheel. She woke early with the sun warming the car through the windshield and stretched lazily. Nothing was open yet, so she rinsed her mouth and face with water from a bottle and went to the pee in the nearby field, hidden by bulrushes and long grass that tickled her knees and soaked her runners with dew. In the phone booth, she found the number for the nearest garage. A young male voice answered on the first ring.

Tory watches the mechanic leave the store and moves to the cash, holding out a five-dollar bill. "Tory, huh?" The owner looks at her and she finally finds a smile in his eyes.

Shrugging, she explains, "My father is a serious Conservative."

As he hands Tory change, her eyes fix on his missing finger.

"I used to like to eat raw meat when I was a boy," he says. "Stuck my hand in the grinder when my big brother wasn't looking and he took it right off." Tory searches his face for a pained expression, but all she finds is laughter. "Believe or believe not," he says.

She smiles, leaves the counter and waves goodbye to the woman, whose call of "good luck" follows her out the door.

The young guy is waiting for her outside, smoking a cigarette. "It's just over there," Tory starts to point towards the gas pump and stops. "I guess you found it," she says, noticing the tow truck already parked in front of the Malibu.

"Yep, they told me you broke down across from Stella Estrella."

"What does that mean anyway?"

"Someone told me it's Star Star in Portuguese and Italian. Or Spanish. I can't remember exactly."

"Star Star."

"Now I got one for you," he gestures to the paint job on the car. In bright, kindergarten lettering, *ZOB* adorns one side, and *MOVE IT* is scrawled across the other.

"Mostly it was just my friend having fun before I left. At first she just liked those letters, later she decided that it meant *Zen Order of Buddhists Move It.*" Tory gives a shrug to his raised eyebrows.

"Where you headed?" he asks, shaking his head.

"West."

"Where west?"

"I don't know."

He nods as if she's just given the correct answer to a question on a game show.

"I had some trouble with the starter," Tory suggests as the young guy opens the hood of the car and tells her to try turning over the engine.

"Hmmm. Well, it ain't driving anywhere like this," he concludes and begins hooking up the station wagon. He jiggles some chains, dusts his hands on his jeans and opens the door to the tow truck for Tory. She jumps in the front seat and shifts around to look at her car. As she turns, Tory notices a woman standing in the doorway of the bakery. Dark hair frames a pale face. The woman's features are like a line drawing, a stark sketch of a person standing in an empty carnival café. In her hands, she holds a rag and a bottle of bright blue window cleaner. Her black eyes look through Tory, their focus fixed far on the horizon. She stands perfectly placed within the middle of the doorframe. Across her chest, the sign on the door still reads *Closed*.

As the tow truck lurches forward, Tory tries to keep the woman in focus, but all she can see is the Malibu bumping along behind them—nose up, snubbing the world—and the town's one billboard that exclaims, *Testicle festival, have a ball!* Tory shifts again to look out the windshield.

She hadn't noticed in the dark last night, but on this road, it seems possible to drive straight into the sky, to become lost in it. Floating, fighting desperately to grasp something, but finding only air, great handfuls of air.

Insomnia

About the same time she decides to grow her toenails, Katherine begins to see bugs. She doesn't see them everywhere, only in her small bachelor apartment. At first, the bugs appear as dark scurrying blurs in her peripheral vision. She turns quickly to get a better look at the movement, to gather proof of the invading creatures, but by the time her eyes focus, everything is still.

Before she moved in, her landlady, Leeta, assured Katherine that the apartment had been fumigated. Leeta is a short woman who always dresses in a white blouse and skirt, with nylon knee-highs and flip-flop sandals on her feet. Her white hair is piled high on her head and held in place by a net. She owns a large white cat that roams the halls and hisses at the tenants. When Leeta showed Katherine the apartment, which was mainly a square containing one closet and a small kitchen area designated by the linoleum on the floor as opposed to the hardwood covering the rest of the room, the old woman led Katherine to the bathroom and sat on the toilet as she talked. Leeta's white skirt rode up above her knees and her generous bottom spread out under her. At first, Katherine thought she was peeing and marveled at her landlady's lack of inhibition. But really, Leeta was simply resting her swollen legs by sitting on the only seat available in the empty apartment. Katherine signed a lease, moved in and, as she unpacked, found ancient, dusty roach hotels under the sink and in the closet.

Roaches. At first, teeny weeny baby ones. Now, great big bugs with hard-shelled backs that clatter across the floor making an unbearable noise that Katherine can't be sure isn't just a figment of her imagination. When Katherine complained to her landlady, Leeta came to her apartment, peered into cupboards and closets, and pronounced, "Clean."

"Do you hear that sound?" Katherine whispered.

As Leeta cocked her head, her white hair shifted like meringue. "No sound," she asserted and left Katherine standing alone in the middle of her room, listening.

At her little table, Katherine covers her ears and skims the Help Wanted ads, beginning with the column marked *Teachers*. In the space of these small squares, she finds the room to dream. Katherine is convinced she'd be good with young children. She remembers many fairy tales and would tell them using funny voices she's sure would make kids laugh. She stares hard at an advertisement for a position as an elementary teacher at Immaculate Conception. Her eyes blur the print on the page. When she focuses again, she is looking under the column entitled *General*. She decides that with her lack of qualifications she has two choices—

Like to listen to rock music?		Adults only.
Need a good job?	or	Female.
I'm hiring 7 new sales		849-8611.
people. Cash bonuses.		
Ask for Jeff 489-3883.		

She circles these ads and then flips to the crossword. The clue, number fourteen across: suffix of song and slug. Katherine pencils in "bird." Song of the slugbird. She smiles, folds the paper carefully and presses her ink-stained fingers to her wrists, leaving four perfect prints on her skin.

She hums a song to herself and waits for Laszlo. When the buzzer rings, she smoothes the wrinkles from her bed, grabs her coat and runs downstairs to meet him.

Laszlo is a messy, smelly boy who's just spent a year working on a sheep farm in New Zealand. Katherine hasn't known him long. She picked him up in a bar and followed him home one night to a cement room in the back of a basement workshop. The air smelled like sawdust and his bed was a pile of coats spread over a futon frame. As he gently eased her onto this nest, she could feel each slat of wood dig into her flesh. They undressed, further padding the bed frame with their own clothes. Katherine was amazed at how she could run her fingers through the hair on Laszlo's back. His hair did not stop at his shoulders, stomach, chest or anywhere for that matter. He was covered in dark curly hair, except for his obviously balding head. His forehead was large and dreadlocks formed a fringe around his ears. But Laszlo didn't care how he looked and neither did Katherine. She grabbed onto him and pulled him closer, deeper.

After, when Laszlo had fallen asleep, Katherine stared at his hand, which lay close to her face. She counted the hairs on his knuckles. She'd gotten to a hundred and sixty-eight before he woke up and shouted, "Zorro!" Laszlo triumphantly scratched a large "Z" across her leg with his toenail. With a queasy stomach, she looked down where a faint impression of the letter remained etched in her dry flaky skin.

Since that night Katherine has restricted their contact to an occasional coffee. Slowly descending her stairs, she sees Laszlo through the glass doors of her apartment building. Jumping up and down, trying to keep warm in the winter wind, his dreads fly in the air as he moves. Katherine joins him outside. He stops bouncing only long enough to give her a sloppy kiss. She tips her head to meet his lips, looks up at the clear bright sky and shivers. Icicles hang from the branches of skeleton trees. The traffic of the city is slowed to a cautious crawl. The sidewalks are slippery. They shuffle over the ice to a nearby coffee shop and take a booth in the corner.

"Baaaa," Laszlo says, swooping in close to Katherine's face. His breath smells like cigarettes and grape juice. Katherine smiles indulgently.

"Baaaaaaaa," Laszlo insists.

"What are you doing?"

"Speaking sheep."

"Oh."

"People assume that one Baaaa is the same as the next." Laszlo jabs the air in Katherine's general direction.

"Really."

"Yeah, but it's a little more complicated than that. The sheep's vocabulary is actually based on four different sounds." Laszlo pauses as the waitress brings their coffee. Katherine leans over her cup, letting the steam warm her face. Her elbows stick to syrup smeared on the table. She feels like an insect caught on flypaper.

Laszlo continues, "The first sound is hunger. The second is the cry of a young sheep looking for its mother. And the third is a nonsense Baaaa, used in general chatter when they have nothing much to say. That's the one I was using when we first sat down."

"What's the fourth?"

"Ahhh, that's a funny thing." Laszlo sips his coffee, taking time to answer. "The final bleat is a cry of freedom that they call out only if they break loose from the flock. BAAA-aaa, BAAA-aaa! Freedom! This, of course, instantly alerts the shepherd and his dog of the escape so the sheep are never free for long." Laszlo begins to bleat, demonstrating each sheep call. When he's finished the restaurant seems too quiet and the waitress is watching them. He leans back with a satisfied grin. Katherine can see nicotine stains between his teeth. She represses the desire to reach over, put fingernail to tooth and scratch the brown away.

They say goodbye on the street. Laszlo tries to extract a promise for a date, which Katherine avoids by slipping on ice and landing on her hip so hard her teeth rattle in her head. Knees still weak, she stops at the corner store to buy today's *Gazette* and, with the bulky paper tucked under her arm, returns home, where a certain persistent order has been imposing itself on Katherine's life.

Her coat forever finds its way to the same hook. Her scarf lies over her coat with the ends hanging at exactly the same length. Dishes are done instantly, a cup never rests in her sink and water taps are turned snugly to guard against vexatious dripping noises. The one window at the far end of the room is cracked open just enough for air. Her slippers are placed gently under the bed with only the smallest hint of their tips peeping out from under her comforter. Her comforter is plumped daily; the corner turned ever so slightly affords a small glimpse of flannel sheets. Towels are stacked—blue, white, burgundy. Soap to the right of the tub. Shampoo to the left. A bathroom with no stray hairs, a desk denying any sign of use, a kitchen devoid of food smells, an undisturbed bed, a room to live without chaos.

The creeping order that is overcoming her home just as surely avoids her regime of personal hygiene. "I haven't washed my hair in days," she told Laszlo over coffee. She felt strangely fascinated, like watching a failed science experiment just before the explosion.

"Sometimes we don't need to wash," Laszlo responded. "Sometimes we just have to live."

"No." Katherine shook her head and thought suspiciously to herself, "I'm not living. I may even be dying." And she is reminded of a car accident. Those eternal moments just after losing control and just before the crash when the world moves slowly, at a distance, pressed against a window, spinning, but suspended, unable to touch or hurt anyone—until that final moment of impact.

❧ ❧

That night, Katherine tells herself a bedtime story to relax. It is a silent tale. From her bed, she stares at the window and watches her thoughts reflected in the frosted black glass.

Once upon a time there was a beautiful young peasant girl. Her father was a miller who boasted to the King that his daughter could spin straw into gold. The King commanded the maiden be brought to him at the palace where he locked the girl into a room filled with straw and a spinning wheel. As soon as the King left, the maiden began to weep for she could not imagine how she was to perform this miracle.

Suddenly, a small man appeared at the window of the cell.

As Katherine imagines this strange apparition squeezing in

through the window, her heart races. She buries herself under the covers and lies awake in the dark. It's late. The marching band of bugs seems to finally be taking a break. Her eyes itch and burn, but it's better to keep them open because when she closes her eyes, small noises grow large. Her pulse becomes a helicopter, the sound of her hair against the pillow is a hissing snake and her thoughts are a loud echo across a vast canyon. She picks at her anxiety like a scab.

◖ ◗

Katherine left Andrew for no good reason. That is, according to Andrew. Katherine knew he simply couldn't understand her abandoning a successful architect, a beautiful downtown apartment and the chance of marriage for an impoverished independence.

Katherine's frail, almost ethereal appearance attracts men who like to wind their hands in her fine blonde hair, pull her head back and expose her white neck to the sky.

"As far as I'm concerned you do not shit," was Andrew's first command in their new home. "You can piss, but I never want to know that you shit."

"What are you talking about?" Katherine laughed before she realized he was serious.

"I'm talking about the fact that you do not shit. It can be done. I lived with Beth for five years without ever smelling or hearing her shit." Andrew's whole body shuddered.

"Can *you* shit? I mean is it just me or is it you, too?" Katherine still couldn't believe he meant what he said.

"Enough of that." He ignored her questions and turned his back to finish unpacking his books. Books filled with designs of cells and classrooms. Andrew specialized in schools and prisons.

Although she couldn't even pretend to understand Andrew's demands, Katherine decided to try her best. She liked when Andrew was pleased with her. His jaw would relax, his shoulders drop, his hands unclench. The sight of a fist, even one resting on a book, made Katherine nervous. Too many nights she'd stared at her father's hands, wondering what they would do. Sometimes they'd stay closed, a glass clutched in the centre of his tight grip. "Gut rot," he called his preferred drink of rye. When his hands were on his glass, Katherine could trust them; they wouldn't move until the bottle was empty. When the bottle was empty, Katherine tried hard to disappear, but a small house, even if you are a small girl, offers a limited range of hiding.

Except for his rigid hands, Andrew did not seem to be anything like her father. Educated, successful, on his way up—so different from the other boyfriends she'd had—when Katherine met Andrew she could see a life she was missing. She had thought Andrew could provide her with a purpose, a feeling of safety, a reliable fuck, a shoulder to lean on, a stable home, a sense of being and a sense of being with another. In the end, Andrew had provided her with everything she thought he could. For a time.

◖◗

"Never did and never will, just the way it's always been." The morning light splashes against Katherine's closed eyes as she mouths the words to a song. She reaches to turn the alarm off an hour before it's set to ring. Did she dream? Did she even sleep? No matter. She still feels she could stay in bed a lifetime, cocooned in blankets. If she waits long enough, perhaps metamorphosis will occur. But she has to get up. Yesterday, when she called about the telemarketing position, they hired her over the phone. She inches out of bed, avoids the bathroom mirror and arrives at her new sales job promptly at nine o'clock.

The floor manager, Jeff, a pimply blond boy, shows her to a desk. She sits in an orange chair that pitches her backward with a shocking motion. Once she has stabilized herself by perching delicately on the edge of the seat's flattened cushion, Jeff hands her a list of potential clients.

"The job's pretty straightforward. You've got the numbers to call there and this is the script you use to sell the service. Stick to the script. It's been written specifically to get people to want to have their carpets cleaned. They put a lot of time and money into writing the script, so use it. It's there to help you. Questions?"

"Who are they?"

Jeff looks confused.

"You know, 'they.'" Katherine mimes quotation marks in the air, leans forward and almost falls out of her chair. "You know, the people who write the scripts, The people who put a lot of time and money into it. Who are *they*?"

"I dunno." Jeff edges away from her. "If you need me I'll be in there." He points to a small cubicle at the far end of the room, but walks away in the opposite direction, disappearing through another door.

Katherine picks up the list of potential customers and scans it while stealing glimpses of the co-worker whose desk faces hers. The worker stretches a hand towards her and introduces himself. "Hey, I'm JD." When he removes his hand from hers, he self-consciously touches his shaved head and fiddles with the two large silver studs piercing the front of his scalp.

He picks up his phone and punches out numbers. Katherine lifts her own phone to her ear and dials. "Hello," an older woman with a tremulous, fragile voice answers.

Fumbling with her script, Katherine clears her throat. "Um, yes, I'm calling you today to talk about a very special promo- tion . . ."

"We don't want any," the woman's voice still trembles, but she hangs up forcibly enough.

At ten forty-five, Katherine takes her coffee break and meets two other employees. A seventeen-year-old high school student who smells like watermelon Bubble Yum tries to encourage Katherine by telling her that all the clients are "cheap mother- fuckers who shouldn't get you down." Spit flies from her mouth as she speaks. "My name is Jen," she says. "And this is Jean- François." She points to a skinny pale creature with mud- puddle eyes who says nothing.

At eleven, Katherine returns to her desk to make more calls and is hung up on every time. Soon she is slamming the phone into its receiver. JD gives her a sympathetic look, but Katherine feels angry. Jealousy wells up in her as she watches him make sales and fill in order forms. Everyone in the room seems to be having more success than Katherine.

At eleven-twenty, a customer finally sounds interested. "Can I have your full name and address please?"

"Name's Elvis, honey. Like the king."

"OK, Elvis. Your last name, please."

"You sound real sweet. How old are you? Sixteen? Fifteen, maybe?"

"Sir, your last name." She doesn't like the softening of his voice.

He whispers, "I'll bet you got a nice tight ass. A tight pussy, too. Are you a virgin?"

Katherine gently hangs up and carefully raises herself from her tricky seat. Through clenched teeth, she politely says goodbye to JD, Jen and Jean-François. The door slams behind her and she runs down the thirteen flights of stairs to ground level. Her right ear is hot from the constant pressure of the phone being jammed against it as she dialed number after number trying to convince people to have their rugs cleaned by a Carpet Doctor Specialist.

Sweat runs down her back, tickling her skin. As she nears her neighbourhood, she hears a loud BAA-AAA-AAA-ing sound coming at her from behind. It grows increasingly louder as Laszlo runs up to meet her. He leaps in front of her, his eyes wide, his mouth open. Under her breath, Katherine curses. His sounds upset her. Her stomach feels vaguely sick, or maybe it is more her bowels, some place deeper, darker than a belly, some place where substances form and sit and wait.

"Hey, what's up?" Laszlo has stopped bleating.

Katherine's gaze slides off his face down the street towards her apartment building. "Nothing much, just came from a new job." She stares at a house with a bright red door. It is the only spot of colour in a line of buildings, and it looks violent against the grey walls and the dirty snow.

"How was the job?"

"Not bad."

"Want to go for a coffee?"

"I got things to do."

"That's cool. Want to learn a sheep call?" The baaaa starts deep in Laszlo's throat and lasts a long time. "Come on. It's a real release." He urges Katherine to try.

She looks around the empty street and makes a half-hearted attempt at bleating, but the sound is weak and she isn't satisfied. Laszlo looks disappointed. Her shoulders tense and creep up toward her ears. She shakes them loose, trying to ease the strain in her muscles. "I haven't brushed my teeth since I moved," she tells Laszlo.

"That's good, sometimes we treat ourselves too well," he answers.

"I have to go home now." Her apartment building looms ahead.

Laszlo follows. "Home is a safe, warm place and a mustard sandwich."

She closes her door in his happy face and watches as he walks away slowly. He turns a corner and there is nothing left to see. A vacant street. But still she watches, her forehead pressed against the cool glass, head heavy as if some force pushed her from behind. It seems all she can do is watch, waiting for that final moment of impact.

When Katherine enters her apartment, she checks the digital clock. Not even an hour has passed since she left the telemarketing office. She places her coat, on its hook, taking the time to arrange her scarf over the coat and then sprawls across the floor to count her money. Thirty-two dollars and change. Everything has been pawned now: books, clothes, CDs. She would never call her family for help, having moved away as soon as she could. The more distance between her and her father's long reach, the better. Sometimes when she'd hide from her father, it was her mother who found her, a woman with vacant eyes, eyes for rent. Behind her mother's stare there was a constant shifting, one moment her gaze inhabited by a fawning woman who tucked Katherine into bed, the next a treacherous soul who pretended not to hear, not to see. But mostly, Katherine's mother's eyes were abandoned, windows broken and boarded.

She can't ask Laszlo for money. Even if he had any, she won't let herself owe him anything. And she has no other friends. When she was living with Andrew he'd go out with people and leave her at home, saying, "You like to be alone." He was right. She did. But he also liked her to be alone, waiting for him. His. She absolutely can't call Andrew.

When she left Andrew, she had asked him if he remembered the time the toilet overflowed. His eyes were filled with stubborn denial. She said, "It wasn't even shit, it was a little tiny turd, and you were furious." Andrew didn't remember. He had been working in his office while Katherine sat on the tub glaring at the perfidious plumbing. As the water in the toilet bowl swirled and rose, dread clenched her gut. If she flushed one more time surely the water would overflow onto the floor. She snapped on the yellow rubber gloves Andrew used to clean the bathroom and fished out pieces of shit, wrapping them in toilet paper and hiding them under the Kleenex and Q-tips that filled the garbage. She snapped off the gloves and surveyed her work. When she went to get Andrew to help fix the toilet his reaction was violent. He slammed his fist into the tiny mirror above the sink. His blood dripped onto the white tile floor. Later, he denied the whole incident even though his left hand still bore a long scar from the tip of his finger to the bottom of his palm.

Katherine holds onto the little pile of money with both her hands.

The sun is rising when she finally sleeps. The bed seems to grab hold of her. She jerks awake and away from its grasp. The sun has just barely risen when she slides out from under the covers. She carefully steps away from the bed. It looks undisturbed. She goes to the washroom, turns the tap on and slurps water through her hands, careful not to get too wet, too clean. She runs her tongue over her teeth, reveling in the rough uneven sensation. Sleep from two nights before still crusts her lashes.

Returning to the main room, Katherine blinks against the light starting to pour in through her window. She drags her bed to the centre of the apartment. Laszlo insists that sleeping east to west is best. Katherine aligns her bed with the poles and whispers a line from a song. "I love you 'cause I hate you."

In the corner where the bed once stood, the dust moves. It darts across the floorboards. The bugs are bigger now. Katherine looks away and shuts her eyes. The dark is no comfort. Outside, the clouds get lighter as the sun rises behind them.

◖ ◗

Katherine plans to answer the second Help Wanted ad early in the day, but she finds it difficult to leave her apartment. When she called the number in the paper, a gruff male voice interrogated her about her age, weight and cup size. "Have to take a look at ya," the voice growled and gave her an address. She has the information in her pocket and knows she should go soon, but first she decides to clean the dust from the corners. Then she stands for a very long time in front of her door before she can move to open it. She's aware she's avoiding what she has to do. Taking long minutes to dress warmly, she clumsily opens the deadbolt with her mittened hand. She inhales deeply before leaving, filling her lungs with the air of her home. Outside, Katherine's breath is shallow. She has to force the cold air into her mouth and she swallows it in tiny gulps. When she passes a running car, the exhaust billows around her face and the taste of gasoline coats her tongue. She spits.

Taking a folded scrap of paper from her pocket, she sits on a bench and reads the directions. A group of young children pass, roped together by a colourful cord. Two women flank them, talking over their heads about the new guy at the community centre. Katherine watches the women critically. She wants to warn them to look out for the kids, who wobble precariously across the snow in their bulky snowsuits. She longs to follow the children, her arms held wide, ready to catch anyone who might fall. When the daycare workers notice her, she attempts a smile, but they avert their eyes and gather the kids closer, steering them away from Katherine.

She lowers her head. When she looks up again, the kids have disappeared, but she sees her landlady standing on the corner dressed in a white winter coat. Leeta's body blends into the large snowdrifts at the side of the road, leaving only her pink face visible, floating above the earth like Wonderland's Cheshire cat. The elderly woman watches the light turn green and steps tentatively from the sidewalk, testing the winter ground in front of her. Katherine's gaze takes in an approaching vehicle. The fast-moving van tries to brake, but its tires lock. Time becomes lethargic and dull. Katherine watches the van point its nose at Leeta and slide slowly, silently on the black ice covering the intersection. She tells herself that now she must move, must call out, must warn Leeta, but finally the time that once seemed so endless rushes forward and leaves no moment for Katherine to act. Leeta looks up, leaves her foot hovering over the ground, and stands still as the van passes her and comes to a stop a safe distance away. She raises a white-gloved fist to the driver and crosses the road, her red face bobbing in the air.

Katherine unfixes herself from the bench and propels herself forward. She fights the panic in her throat, looks again at the address in her hand. Her trip will take her far into the suburbs. She already regrets the bus fare that has to be spent.

The subway ride seems to last forever and, by the time she reaches her destination, it is getting dark again and the panic has returned. Double-checking the address, she hesitates only slightly before walking up a sidewalk to a split-level bungalow. The house looks like any other, with beige siding and dark brown trim. Snow has been carefully cleared from both the driveway and the stairs leading to the door. Katherine rings the bell and a girl in tight jeans and a cut-off T-shirt answers almost immediately.

"You must be the girl who called. I'm Judy," she says and leads Katherine into a living room, where another girl lies on a plaid couch watching a nature program about an ape, Mimi, who communicates through sign language. "Do you want some tea?" Judy asks, gesturing for Katherine to sit down. Katherine sits on the edge of an over-stuffed easy chair and watches Mimi sort through photographs, classifying each as either human or animal. In one pile, the animal has grouped pictures of a deer, an elephant and Donald Duck. In another pile, she has selected photos of Bill Clinton, her trainer, Cindy Crawford and herself.

After only a few minutes, a man walks into the room and shuts off the TV. His arms and neck are thick. His nose looks like it has been moulded from clay and stuck onto his face with glue. He barely looks at Katherine. "The girls will show you around and fill you in on the rules," he grumbles before he leaves.

There are three bedrooms upstairs. When someone is entertaining in a bedroom, the others in the house try to stay in the front room to provide a sense of privacy. The sheets have to be changed. Everyone shares the laundry. If you are caught doing drugs, you're out. Katherine nods. She struggles to keep her mind blank, but the story of Rumpelstiltskin invades her thoughts. *The maiden began to weep for she could not imagine how she was to perform this miracle.*

Katherine follows the girls to the dungeon. The basement is painted black with chains fixed to the walls beside a shelf full of masks, whips and silver needles. "Do you mind doing the dominatrix thing?" Judy looks at Katherine while the other girl hoists herself onto a table that has straps dangling from the sides. She crosses her legs, cocks her head and smiles encouragingly at Katherine.

"I've never done this before."

"Well, if you've got nothing against the dungeon, it can be a good place to start. You're in control and a lot of the time there's no physical contact." Judy notices Katherine's gaze drift to the shelf of tools. "We do use those sometimes, but we'd start you off easy. Any questions?"

Katherine has so many questions she can do nothing but shake her head. Judy squints at Katherine in the dim light. "Are you OK?" She touches Katherine's shoulder.

Katherine shifts away from Judy's touch and thinks, please don't be nice to me. She is relieved when Judy returns to the tour, opening a flimsy sliding door to reveal a washer and dryer set.

"We try to make sure the laundry's done if we know we have a client booked for the dungeon." Katherine nods. Judy quickly transfers a load of wet sheets into the dryer before leading the way back upstairs.

The girls walk Katherine to the front door. Both shake her hand before she leaves. The sky is black, even though it is late afternoon. In the winter, the nights begin early and last a long time. Streetlights reflect off snow and the residential neighbourhood is busy with people returning home from work. They walk with their heads down, their backs hunched over to fight the cold wind. When they open the doors to their homes, they straighten and enter the warmth standing tall, shoulders back. As Katherine steps away from the house, a vent from the basement blows hot air on her ankles and the clean scent of Bounce fabric softener fills her nose. She breathes easily now. Moves quickly. She feels like she's been given a reprieve.

Walking to the subway, she fingers the handful of business cards the girls have given her. A Touch of Class. Mistress Strap On—bondage, spanking and electric shock. Angela's Night Angels. Centerfold Escorts. X-tasy. Down and Dirty Domination. Dangerous Curves. WWW.D-CURVES.COM. Seventh Heaven. Extreme Excitement. Erotic Fantasy Come True. Call. You won't be disappointed!

When Katherine arrives home, she adds these cards to her small pile of money. Twenty-three dollars and seventy-eight cents.

◀◎ ◎▶

There's been no hot water for days. But Katherine doesn't mind because she has no need for it. Still, she feels as if she should do something, perhaps call Leeta. Ask her to fix the water, make sure she's OK after her near miss with the truck. But Katherine does nothing and is concerned by how self-conscious she has become since living alone. As she sits in the tiny apartment, she feels like there is a surveillance camera hooked up in each corner of the room and that every action is being monitored. The sensation might be interesting, if she thought her watcher was at all intrigued by what she is doing, but instead she gets the impression that her watcher is eating donuts and scratching his hairy belly while he tries to stay awake on the job. Maybe she even hears the thud of his head on his desk as he drifts off to sleep.

Or is that the sound of bugs?

On her bed, Katherine stares at the ceiling, trying to ignore the sound of the bugs, her pulse, the saliva trickling down her throat. She thinks of the imprisoned maiden.

Suddenly, a small man appeared at the window of the cell. He asked the girl why she was crying. Through muffled tears, she explained her problem.

"What will you give me if I spin the straw into gold for you?" The little man stared greedily at the maiden.

"I have nothing to offer." The desperate girl began to weep bitterly.

"Will you give me your first child, if you become queen?"

Thinking that an impossibility, the girl agreed and the little man sat down to work. The maiden awoke in the morning to a room full of gold and a smiling King. "I'm very pleased," he said and led her to another, bigger room filled with twice as much straw. "If you can spin this straw into gold by morning you will be my Queen." The King locked the door as he left and the girl sank to the ground, tears forming in her eyes.

Katherine feels a light caress on her hand. Like a breeze. It tickles. She looks down her arm and sees a dark shape travelling over her skin. She jerks her hand, sending the bug flying to the other side of the room. It disappears.

The phone rings. The sound startles her. She stares at it

vaguely, answering it not out of desire, but out of habit. Laszlo is calling to tell her a story about the circus he visited in India. Before New Zealand, Laszlo was in India, before India, Greece. Laszlo is speaking slowly. "And then the performers came out. Starving elephants. Leprous tigers. And a charmer who was as narrow as his snake. None of this was so special, except for the poodle. A tiny animal with bulging eyes who, when it wasn't jumping through hoops, ran in circles to deny the existence of the crowd gathered to watch."

"Why am I listening to this?" thinks Katherine.

"You remind me of that poodle," Laszlo says after Katherine turns him down for another coffee.

She hangs up brusquely. She's restless. Leeta's cat prowls in the hallway, hissing at the air. Ghosts, maybe. Katherine can smell herself. Suddenly, she has the desire to fuck. Or, more precisely, she has the desire to be fucked. She wants to be pushed up against a wall and entered from behind. She wants it to be anonymous. She does not need to see her lover, but she must be able to smell him. She wants to roam the streets sniffing at men until she finds the right one, whom she will politely ask to follow her into an alley and fuck her from behind. As he moves inside her, she will inhale him like air. After, her hair will catch on the bricks as she pushes away from the wall, not surprised to find herself alone. She has consumed him. Katherine touches herself, but when she can't feel herself, stops. She sings, "I wish I would have met you, but now it's a little late."

She wonders if perhaps her sleepless nights are affecting her more than she knows, but is not convinced. "Maybe it's all a lie. Sleep is overrated. Who needs it? I feel fine and I haven't slept a wink for seventy-two hours," Katherine tells herself viciously and looks out the window. Across from her building, people mill in and out of the bakery. They look small and greedy, breaking off pieces of their baguettes to shove into their mouths as they walk. "Fools." Katherine feels superior, powerful.

❦

When the man with the voice of gravel calls from the suburbs, she is grateful and tells herself the waiting is the worst part, she needs this job. When she lived with Andrew, she did not work. She had just been fired from a waitressing job in an Italian pasta and cappuccino bar. The owner was a Catholic family man who wouldn't let her wear short skirts. She had to buy a new outfit for the job. Every time she put on the green coatdress and white open-toe sandals she felt like she was playing dress-up. When Katherine caught the owner watching her through a peephole in the washroom, he fired her.

Andrew encouraged her to relax. He pointed out that she wasn't a good waitress and there was no need for her small income. Besides, he added, a good thing had come from the job—she'd met him there. During her shift, he'd often come to the restaurant with a date. One evening, he arrived at closing time alone and the next week they were looking for apartments. He wanted something bigger anyway and it just made sense that Katherine move in. When she lost her job, Andrew suggested that maybe she could go to school again. Do that Education certificate she was always talking about. Not this year, but maybe the next.

One day Katherine brought home a calendar from the community college. That evening she showed it to Andrew, who stood over her, hands clenched. Katherine stared at his white knuckles and saw that he was holding a fist full of promises he would never let go. As his hand came down with a thud on the table in front of her, she felt the threat inching closer and knew it wouldn't be long before he became more honest with his fist.

Sitting by her window, Katherine's gaze shifts to the paint on the frame. Purple. Violet. Blue. The colour of a bruise. A dark spot scurries across the sill. Her arm darts out and she cups her hand over the bug. Her face goes hot. She doesn't want to look. Blood pounds in her ears, but she still thinks she can hear the soft tap dance of the trapped creature. Ever so slightly, she lifts her thumb and peeks into the small dark cave. Nothing.

She lifts her whole hand. The purple paint seems to turn a brighter shade, her apartment blushes.

The phone rings again. She ignores it, letting the answering machine pick it up. Laszlo leaves a message. "Hi, Katherine. I think you phoned here a few days ago, but the time and place for coffee was unclear. Call me back." Katherine moves to the washroom to prepare herself. The last part of the message is drowned by the sound of running water. She catches the final phrase and repeats it to herself, working the words in her mind. "Place for coffee was unclear, space for coffee unclear, space for coffee is male, space for people is male, space people read your mail. Call me back." Click. Mmmmmmmmmmmm.

She holds her hands under the taps for a long time before she remembers the hot water is broken. The shower is ice cold, but Katherine forces herself into it. "Go on, take everything, take everything, I want you to . . ." she screams out a song as she lathers soap over her whole body, shampoos her hair and cuts her toenails. Had she really decided to let them grow? It seems impossible, a time when she had enough energy to actually make a decision.

By the time she begins shaving her legs, she's shivering and covered in goose bumps. The razor snags on her frozen skin and small pinpoints of red start to form. She steps from the shower cleaner, but bloodier. She twists the cap off a new tube of toothpaste and brushes her teeth.

An hour later, the peppermint taste still lingers in her mouth as Judy greets her at the door a second time. "Hey girl." Judy's smile is wide, pleasant. "You clean up good."

Without the layer of filth, Katherine feels exposed. She believed no one could see her tangled hair, dirty nails and crusted eyes because she'd been thinking of herself as an invisible woman. "Thanks," she says shyly.

"Let me take your coat."

"Thanks."

The house is quiet, there isn't even the distant murmur of the television. "It's a slow night," Judy says and leads the way into the front room. "How are you feeling?" She sounds more like a guidance counselor than a prostitute.

"Nervous, I guess," Katherine answers what she thinks is the appropriate response. She doesn't want to explain that she is without sensation, like a limb that's fallen asleep, she can poke and pinch, but doesn't even feel a tingle.

"It's to be expected. Just remember, down in the dungeon, it's all a mind game and you're in control."

Katherine fights the urge to laugh. Her eyes roll in her head a bit. Maybe now she is tired? Too late. She's vigilant, patrolling the border between sleep and wakefulness.

The doorbell rings and Katherine jumps. Judy smiles. "That's him. You go downstairs and put on the little black suit in the laundry room. I'll bring him down in a couple of minutes and stay with you to get things started. Then I'll slip away." Judy nudges Katherine to the stairs as the door rings again.

Katherine descends carefully, gliding her hand down the rail for guidance. The darkness is complete. She rounds the corner into the main room, where candles are lit. Their flames barely move in the still air. She can hear Judy and another deeper voice talking from some place that seems very far away. She opens the sliding door and sees her outfit hanging above the dryer. Shedding her own mini skirt, she struggles into a skin-tight, fake leather jumpsuit that smells like Eternity. She rearranges her breasts to fit into the designated cups and takes a deep breath. When she exhales she accidentally blows out two candles. There are footsteps on the stairs. The voices get louder.

Judy enters the room and calmly looks at Katherine, who tries a smile. But when no one else smiles, Katherine lets her mouth relax. Judy quietly shuts the door to the laundry room and motions for the man to sit on the table. Now he grins. He seems fairly young and wears a suit the colour of buttered mashed potatoes. When he turns toward the table, Katherine sees that his shirt tag is sticking up at the back of his neck and the cuffs of his pants are dirty from the winter slush outside.

"You have my permission to take off your clothes now,"

Judy instructs, watching Katherine to make sure she's paying attention. The man undresses. "Lie down." Judy's voice is a low monotone. At her cue, Katherine fastens the man's wrists with two straps, carefully avoiding his eyes. Judy tightens them until his skin puckers under the bindings.

Judy takes a small whip from the shelf and trails the tip across his skin, lightly, like the softest loving touch. Then she cracks it loudly against the table. Katherine winces. Judy looks bored. Her chin drops close to her neck, her mouth turns downward, her eyes blink rapidly. She's stifling a yawn.

The room is growing hot. Just when Katherine thinks she's been forgotten, Judy hands her the whip and quietly climbs the stairs. The whip is slick from Judy's sweaty palm. It slips from Katherine's hands. When she bends to pick it up, she feels the man's foot on her ass. His toe nudges her insistently. She straightens quickly and slaps his foot away. He makes a satisfied sound, an encouraging *mmm* that feels wet in Katherine's ear.

She watches her arm rise slowly in the air. The candles' flames flicker with her movement, a languid dance of light against the dark wall. Time suspended. Then she is released. Her hand easily slices the air. The moment the leather strap strikes skin, she's struck by the impact. Her palm tingles. When she raises the whip she sees a red welt already forming across his pale skin. She feels him staring at her. Her eyes move up his body, taking in every small detail. His chest is slightly sunken and in the middle there is a dent that looks especially vulnerable. A thin sheen of sweat covers his skin. He has a few grey hairs under his arms and there is a small patch of stubble beneath his chin, which he missed with his razor this morning. Other than that, his face is smooth and flushed. She looks into his eyes. He shows her his teeth and says, "Please."

She pulls her arm back to strike again, but stops. The whip drops to the ground. Katherine's skin burns. She blinks the sweat from her eyes and, when her vision clears, she is surprised by her surroundings. She's not exactly sure how she arrived at this place. She feels stupid. She tells herself she's not.

"Come on." The man's voice is jarring. She hears the strap rattle against the table as he struggles with his bonds. "Come on. Come on." Katherine has the impression that he's praying. She reaches back and frees one of his hands. He grabs hold of himself. Katherine knows she does not exist for him any more. She stares into the darkness of the stairway and listens to him over the sound of her own pounding heart.

When the room becomes silent, she approaches the table and undoes the second strap. He rubs his wrist and reaches for tissue to mop up the shiny trail of semen crossing his lower stomach like a pale, iridescent worm. The man dresses unhurriedly, pausing over each shirt button. He watches her. She once again avoids his eyes. He clears his throat. "Do you want to know my name?" he asks. She shakes her head, but as he passes her on his way out he stops, tucks her fine hair behind her ear, leans in, and whispers his name against her exposed throat.

Franz. His breath is warm and moist, and Katherine feels a trembling. She looks around, but nothing else moves, it is only her bones that are shaking. By the time he finally climbs the stairs, Katherine is exhausted. The tension has eased from her body, leaving only a heavy fatigue. As she slowly strips off her tight black suit, the acrid smell of sweat burns her nostrils. In her mouth, the fresh peppermint taste has been replaced by thick sour saliva. She carefully hangs up the jumpsuit. Every small action takes especially long because of her clumsy fingers.

Her clothes, lying in a pile by the washer, look unfamiliar to her. She squats to find her underwear. When she stands up, she sees something on the ground between her feet. She backs up and drops to her knees. Her eyes narrow in disbelief.

In front of her on the shag rug there is a small, perfectly round piece of shit. It is fresh. Warm. She looks around the room, searching for answers, but the dark corners remain silent, seeming to point in her direction. She feels like the room is accusing her.

She dresses hastily, suddenly chilled. An outline of the man still remains on the sheet covering the table. She pulls this off, rolls it up and sticks it in the washer. She returns the whip to the shelf and gathers the man's discarded tissues, using them to pick up her shit, which she carefully places in the garbage on top of the Bounce sheets and clumps of lint. Not hidden. A dark mark revealed on a bed of white.

Judy calls from upstairs.

"Coming," Katherine answers, taking one last look at the room. It is tidy and still. It almost looks as if she was never there. She climbs the dark stairs two at a time.

"How was it?" Judy asks, holding out four wrinkled twenty-dollar bills.

Katherine looks at the money in her hands. "I cleaned up and put the sheet in the washer."

"That's fine." Judy guides her to the living room and repeats, "How was it?"

"Not bad."

Judy looks at her and snorts. "Yeah right! Of course it was bad," she says. "It couldn't have been good. What I mean is, how are you?"

"I'm trying not to think about it."

"Maybe that's a good thing."

"Maybe."

"There are other options, you know. You don't have to come back." Judy's arms hang loosely at her sides.

Katherine folds her arms across her chest, hugging herself. She asks, "Options?" She says it like a foreign word. One that can be articulated, but not deciphered.

Judy's speech blurs and Katherine excuses herself to go home.

The soft rocking motion of the subway lulls Katherine into a light sleep. When she enters her apartment she has forgotten Judy, the house and the man. She hardly notices the red light on her answering machine blinking red, call me, red, call me back. In the bathroom, the toothpaste lies in the sink, oozing mint. Hair clogs the drain. She hears noises in the hallway. Leeta's cat, creeping. At the table, Katherine is aware that if she lifts her gaze even a fraction, she will be looking directly outside. In the street, the sense of people waking and shifting is almost tangible. The sun shines brightly, warming her arm as she swoops down to crush a bug with her bare hand. "Oh yes," Katherine thinks, a dry smile splitting her face.

She feels strangely optimistic and eagerly climbs under the covers of her bed. The little troll man appears.

A year has passed and the little man visits the maiden, who is now Queen. She is nursing her baby with a sweet expression on her face until she sees her visitor and understands his threat. When she weeps, the little man offers her hope, though he is smugly confident in his game. Tomorrow night he will return and if she can guess his name, he will release her from her promise.

That night the Queen sends her men to find the little man's name. One soldier returns and whispers "Rumpelstiltskin" in her ear.

This is the happy ending.

Katherine's comforter feels heavy on her sore, tense muscles. The Queen keeps her baby. And the little man stomps his foot so hard he crashes through the floor. Katherine twists and turns, and then frantically kicks the quilt off the bottom of the bed, emerging from her cocoon of covers. But, the Queen is still married to a man who would kill her for gold. Katherine lies awake. She closes her eyes. She opens her eyes. It makes no difference. She stares through darkness and hums a song to herself.

The Woman Who Sat by the Sea

She moved through the water, breathing liquid, seeing blue, Technicolor blue, with streaks of golden fish sailing by. Then she was falling over fire, trees on fire. When she landed, she died.

‹❨ ❩›

Before consciousness, there was pain. An ache that began in the woman's throat like a scream. Her eyes opened, she saw nothing. As she tried to breathe the scalding air, the dust of ashes dried her mouth. Then shapes began to form and focus. The forest was alive with deadly things. Smoke curling from the tips of their branches, blackened trees stood tall like gunfighters firing pistols into the sky. Roots snaked across the ground. Steam rose everywhere, ghosts who danced and swayed and seared her eyes until she was forced to close them tightly. Darkness again. Silence. The cracking and snapping of the fire had long ago died. Though she could feel the breeze slicing her skin, the wind was mute, having no leaves or grass to rush through.

She felt the sound before she heard it. First, an itch deep within her ears. Then, the buzz of a bee. Finally, the roar of a small airplane. The woman jerked upright, as water splashed down over the charred forest. She felt her skin rip across her flesh while she watched the plane sweep upward and away. The sky was empty again. The woman looked at her body, now clean from the soot and dirt and bits of cloth. Red, blistered skin, tender to touch. Smell of burnt hair. Trying to breathe the scalding air, she eased herself to her feet and began to walk in the direction of the disappeared plane.

She moved slowly, concentrating only on where her next step should be placed. The floor of the forest was still hot, the ash damp from the efforts of the firefighting plane. As all the brush and undergrowth had been burned away, her only obstacles were fallen branches and broken trees. Coming to a small stream, she bent for a drink. The water was cold and tasted like apples. She sat there for a long time, tired even though behind her she could still see the spot where she had lain. As she rested, the woman realized that her feet felt soothed from the cool mud of the shore, so she scooped large handfuls of it onto her body, covering her legs, belly, breasts, arms and, finally, her head and face.

As she caught sight of her reflection in the clear water, she struggled hard to recognize herself, to recall her name. Her questions were met with a blank mind. When she stood again, she felt heavier but more comfortable. Much relieved in her camouflage suit, she named herself Charlene. Char for short, she decided with a little smile. Her lips felt tight and sore under the mud. She let her face go slack, gingerly jumped over the stream and kept walking.

When night came, Char rested, filled with hunger. She consumed her sleep, fed off her dreams. A delicious tomato, ripened on the vine, heavy with juice, sliced onto fresh warm rye bread. Mangoes. Suddenly swimming—years had come and gone, the sound of metal. Then falling.

❦

It was not quite light yet. The sky was a deep blue, instead of black, and towards the east there was a softening. On the horizon, Char could see treetops. The sight motivated her to move from her resting spot, a shallow hole she had dug in the ground, which had sheltered her from the wind and kept her balm of mud moist and cool over her burnt skin. During the night, worms had slid over her. In the morning, she shook herself free from the earth.

The sun climbed in the sky and winked at Char with the passing of each cloud. Finally reaching the border of the burnt area, Char stepped away from the dead forest and disappeared into the lush green foliage not touched by flames. Walking through the woods provided its own challenge. The brush was thick and deep, forcing Char to stop and bind her feet with dried reeds for protection. And, where the site of the fire had been eerily silent, this new terrain offered an abundance of sounds. Leaves rustled overhead as squirrels jumped from treetop to treetop. Wind moved through the bushes. Small creatures shook the grass. But most amazing, were the thousands of small birds perched in the branches, kissing the sky with their songs.

Char's attention was soon captured by the vision of large ripe blackberries. She hurried to the bush and eagerly shoved the fruit into her mouth. Briars caught and scratched at her fingers and wrists as she plucked handfuls of berries. Her mouth filled with juice. Small seeds stuck in her gums. The taste of blood and mud mingled with the sweet wine taste of the fruit. She ate until her stomach cramped, wiped her soiled hands on the mossy forest floor and moved on.

She kept walking until the sun sank and a full low-hanging moon shone brightly on the forest. Char wanted to continue, but she felt like she could bang her head on that moon, so she was forced to stop for the night. Digging her bed, she tried to remember the day before she awoke in the forest. She had sipped cinnamon coffee in the morning and eaten toast with butter and sugar on top. Had she gone swimming? She moved through the water like she was standing still. It seemed as though years had come and gone. Then, she was sucked up into darkness. She could feel the walls of her confinement and pounded on these walls with clenched fists.

◖◗

In the morning, Char ate green hazelnuts. She peeled the prickly skin off the nut, cracked the unripe shell with her teeth and chewed on the soft tasteless seed inside. It took her a very long time to eat enough nuts to be satisfied.

Char could feel her cloak of mud stiffen with the warmth of the sun. Whereas the cold at night was carnivorous, biting at her flesh and eating into her sleep, the warmth of the day was benevolent, like the large rough tongue of a cow warming her skin with long slow licks. Becoming drowsy with this heat, Char shook herself awake and decided it was time to move on again. Though her destination was not clear, some instinct pushed her forward. Soon she broke through the woods and faced green sloping hills.

The air was more humid here. Long grass rippled in the wind and dandelion seeds with downy tufts swirled against the blue sky. Char bent and plucked a wish from the ground. Holding the flower between her fingers, she closed her eyes, brought the white cloud close to her lips and blew. The fuzz from the dandelion drifted away and Char was left holding a stem with a bald head.

She opened her eyes. The breeze still played in the grass. The sun had not moved. Char let the dandelion fall to the ground and started to climb the first hill. Her movement was efficient, deliberate steps that covered ground with purpose.

That night, when she stopped, she smelled the sea in the distance and the rolling hills became water lapping against her body. She moved through the water, breathing liquid. Her hands and feet were fins.

In the day, she swam over the hills. No longer did she have to fight to take a step through bushes and trees. She could walk unhampered, but was careful to avoid the small farms and the people travelling on dirt roads. At one time, she had hoped for rescue, but now Char didn't need the help of anyone. She was convinced that her tongue was dirt and would crumble if she were forced to talk. In fact, she felt like her whole being was the soil she wore and the ground was more kin to her than the people she glimpsed.

These people seemed unreal. Hair combed. Clothed in dresses and pants and shirts and too much stuff. Talking sounds that needn't be said. Everything was excess to Char. She could not stop. She swam over the hills—until she stubbed her toe on a very large rock.

Char stood at the base of the very large rock and looked up, way up, to where something swayed and bumped high against the stone. A man. Two men, climbing the rock and talking about how good their sandwiches were going to taste once they got to the top. Char ducked down and scooted to the other side, watching the sun glance off the sweaty backs of the rock climbers. She felt desire as she watched the men, muscles pulling and rubbing under their skin. These were beautiful men wearing tight, brightly coloured pants that made Char think of fish. And the sea.

Past the rock, far in the distance, Char could see tall buildings, their outline hazed by the cover of smog. By tomorrow, she would reach this city, which she felt must be her home. And she still wasn't sure how she had ever left. She had been swimming, diving far under the ruckus of the waves. She had heard the sound of a motor getting louder and louder. There was darkness. The water tasted like iron.

Char stood scared and cold in the bright beautiful daylight. The rock climbers had disappeared over the edge of the cliff. The sun was high in the sky, stabbing her eyes with brilliant rays. She could hear crickets rubbing their legs together, making a song that buzzed too deeply in her ears. Her stomach was empty, but no longer rumbled with hunger. It fed off itself. Dry grass scratched her legs, but she couldn't find the energy to move.

Char curled into herself and slept, hidden by the grass. When she opened her eyes, it was dark and lightning bugs flashed across the sky, stars close enough to touch and catch and hold in her hands like a wish.

She felt strong again and sunrise found her leaving the dirt roads of the country to follow a highway into the city. People stared at her from their cars, but they moved so quickly she was soon forgotten or thought to have been imagined. Nobody could really believe the sight of Char striding purposefully beside the highway, eyes shining white against her cloak of mud.

On entering the maze of buildings, however, people could no longer blink her away. They looked at her strangely and started to follow her through the streets.

Char walked on, not unaware of the attention, but completely unaffected. Her plan was to reach the water, hear its lullaby and know she was finally home. As she rounded one last corner, she escaped the city and there before her lay the sea. Suddenly relieved, grateful and exhausted, Char sank to the ground and sat on the sun-drenched sand. The tide was out, the waves crested far from the boardwalk. Just a little rest, and then she was going to enter the water and let the salt waves heal her skin. She wanted to float in those waves for eternity. But first, just a little rest.

⊂⦿ ⦿⊃

As the sun reached its peak in the sky, Char sat by the sea while people gathered and shifted behind her. They asked questions amongst themselves. Who was she? Where did she come from? Why does she sit here? If they had asked Char, she would have replied.

She had been swimming. Her hands and feet cut the waves like fins. Air strapped to her back, she moved through the water and seemed to breathe the liquid. The sea was blue, Technicolor blue, with streaks of golden fish sailing by. She moved like she was standing still. It seemed as though years had come and gone.

She'd felt the sound before she heard it. An itch deep within her ears. A shadow, a roar, and then she was sucked up into darkness. She could feel the walls of her confinement and pounded on these walls with clenched fists. The sound of metal shook her blood. The water tasted like iron. And then she was falling over fire, trees on fire.

When she landed, she died. The water around her boiled and became steam. She couldn't breathe the fire.

But no one asked a single question of the woman herself.

The woman, herself, drowsed in the warmth of the day, glad to not be moving, moving, moving. The sound of the waves rushed over Char. The smell of salt and fish filled her nose. Even with her eyes closed, she could still see the water. She smiled and felt the sun dry her cloak of mud.

∾ ∾

Later, when the people realized Char had not moved in hours, they were concerned, went home confused and had the nagging feeling they had lost something. They patted their pockets, thinking perhaps they had forgotten a valuable trinket in their clothes. They walked from room to room, staring blankly at walls and in cupboards, trying to remember why they had stirred in the first place.

The next day, after a good night's sleep, people forgot they had seen the woman walk up and sit down by the boardwalk. They praised the city for this beautiful new statue, which would disappear under the waves with the coming of the tide and emerge newly polished each time the water retreated. The people of the city insisted a gold plaque be made where they could engrave her name or a few words describing this woman. In the end, though, nobody knew her story and the plaque remained blank. A shining, golden rectangle nestled under the figure of the woman sitting by the sea.

The Perfect Vacation

Pat started her daily routine with a cold shower. She liked the shock of freezing water on her sleep-warmed body. Each morning, as she poked her feet out from under her comforter and pushed them into her fuzzy slippers, she would anticipate the moment when her breath caught in her throat and her heart stopped for just one instant. Fresh from the shower, she would slip on white cotton underwear and sit at her kitchen table with a coffee and an oven-toasted chocolate croissant. She hardly ever read a newspaper. Instead, she wrapped her cold hands around her warm cup and watched the world outside her window. Tall elm trees lined the sidewalks. Neighbours talked to each other over fences and children played hockey in the street, stopping mid-game to move the goalie nets aside each time a car passed. After licking the last of the buttery pastry off her fingers, she would return to her bedroom, put on her work clothes and head out the door. This morning was no different except that, for the first time since starting her own business, she did not have to go to work. Pat was on vacation.

This Monday morning, she sat at her kitchen table in her bra and panties, sucked melted chocolate from the middle of a croissant, stared out her window and felt as if she could not move from her kitchen table. When the mailman came at ten thirty, she had to duck and hide behind the counter in order to avoid giving him a free show. Jolted from her languor, she made her way to the bedroom to dress. As she passed her small sitting room, Sister Polly cried out, "Call me a lawyer. Innkeeper, a drink. Amen! Hallelujah!"

Pat shook her head. She had even forgotten to uncover Sister Polly. She entered the room, drew back yellow flowered curtains and moved towards a large cage. One black eye stared at her through a hole in the old blanket that covered the cage. "Hello, sweetie. Did you have a good sleep? Would you like some water?"

The parrot shifted onto its swing, shook its red tail feathers and responded, "A banana?"

"No. Water?"

"Banana."

"Later. For now, some water and sunflower seeds."

"Banana!"

"That's enough, Sister Polly. Calm down." She touched the ravaged area on the bird's neck where Sister nervously plucked out feathers. Pat liked the feel of the occasional pinfeather sticking out of the parrot's soft, wrinkly skin.

"Pat?"

"Yes, Sister Polly, it's Pat. How are you?"

"How are you?"

"I'm fine. Now eat your breakfast."

Pat closed the living room door with a sigh, blocking out Sister Polly's final insistent demand for "Banana!"

"Banana, banana," she murmured to herself, as she pulled on a pair of jeans and selected a T-shirt from a stack of identical white tops.

She had bought the parrot last year, around the same time she'd started her own business. Sister Polly came from breeders who were avid Billy Graham fans. When Pat brought her new pet home, she discovered that the bird's only vocabulary was "amen" and "hallelujah." Keeping with the religious theme, she decided to call the parrot Sister Polly. A month later, when Sister had to go to the vet, Pat was told that her parrot was actually a male bird, but by then the name had stuck. And now, even though Sister had forgotten much of his original religious zeal and knew over two hundred words, he persisted in repeating "banana" enough times to drive his owner over the edge.

Pat had acquired the parrot because she wanted to be responsible for something besides herself. She couldn't imagine having children yet, so she saw Sister as a sort of starter family. At first, she readily gave the bird all the attention he demanded, but now she found herself resenting his exigent nature, which reminded her of the constant obligations of running her own business.

In the beginning, High Flying Balloons had been the challenge she craved. She enjoyed being busy seven days a week, consumed by the responsibilities of a new shop owner. The first year is the hardest. Pat had heard that enough times, from her loan officer to her *New Business* magazines to the customers who came in and bought a bag of balloons for $1.50, wishing her luck but shaking their heads as they left. Pat heaved a great sigh. A year could pass so quickly she hardly knew what had happened to the time. The store, once viewed as a chance for independence, had become a thing to escape. Taking this time off was less a holiday than it was a mad dash for the door. She needed something to happen. But faced with the reality of free time, a minute seemed more like an hour as a full two weeks of nothing to do stretched in front of her.

Suddenly she remembered the mailman and strode toward her front entrance. She pulled open the heavy wood door to her small cottage and walked out into the day, relieved. Following the stone path that led to the sidewalk, she happily noted that her lawn had to be mowed and the weeds trimmed. At the sidewalk, she bent down to pull a dandelion from a crack in the pavement and then straightened to look at her mailbox. She smiled at the colourful scene painted on the sides. At first glance, it looked as though Jersey cows grazed in green fields, their udders shining pink against the metal of the box, but on closer inspection, the cows were revealed as spotted pigs, a strange anomaly that made Pat happy. She'd always liked when things were not as they appeared.

Opening the box's small door, she saw one single slip of paper resting in the dark cavern. Pat fished out a postcard and hurried back inside.

"Screeeeech. Pop. Hello!" Sister Polly imitated the sound of the door opening whenever anyone entered and never failed to call out a cheerful greeting. "Banana!"

"Yeah, yeah," Pat capitulated and went to the kitchen to slice a piece of the sweet fruit for her bird. "This will shut you up a little." She put the banana next to the bars of the cage, where Sister Polly reached for it and immediately spat it out. The parrot looked at her, expectation written across his face.

"Pat?"

"I hate it when you do that, you know?" But she stretched her fingers in through the bars and scratched the bird's head anyway. She knew Sister was just trying to get her attention. "You poor thing," she crooned. Sister rolled his eyes in ecstasy.

Pat sat by the cage and looked at the card in her hand. The image on the front was a spoof of fifties culture, a brightly coloured scene of a perfect family sitting down for dinner. The mother was standing, wearing a red and white apron, and was serving her husband. He looked like Dick Van Dyke and was beaming at his two children, a boy and a girl, both identically blonde. "Meatloaf Night" was printed across the top of the card in blood red.

Pat turned the card over and stared at the message written neatly on the back. It began with a little joke—*It's here! Wish you were beautiful!*—and continued with some fairly boring news about the weather and Sister Polly. It ended in an exclamation—*I can't believe Nan is getting married!*

⟪ ☙ ⟫

Pat's grandmother was ninety-two years old, lived a block away from her and was always good for a hug. Her nan's house was the exact same layout as Pat's, but smelled of apples, cinnamon and beer. Nan had started brewing her own when she was ninety. Since she only drank one beer a week, on Sunday after church, two years worth of stock had accumulated in the old woman's home. Everywhere Pat looked she could see brown bottles stashed, their original labels carefully scrubbed off.

Last week, Nan had had a surprise for her granddaughter. Pat arrived at Nan's just as the older woman was putting her homemade pickles on the table. The younger woman took the jar and forced it open with all her strength. It gave a gratifying popping sound and soon Pat was digging into the pickle juice, trying to scoop out the yellow beans her nan always added in between the cucumbers. Nan slid grilled cheese sandwiches out of a frying pan onto their plates, sat down and then got up again. She returned with a bottle of beer.

"We're celebrating," she explained, as she opened the bottle and poured them each half a glass.

"What are we celebrating?" Pat searched her nan's face. The old woman's eyes were almost hidden by folds of flesh that had long ago drooped down all around her face. She had the look of a hound dog except that her skin was so pale it was almost translucent and her eyes were still brilliantly blue. She raised her glass in a steady hand and smiled secretively.

"What? What are we celebrating, Nan? Tell me."

"I'm pregnant." Nan chortled at her own joke. Her dentures shifted forward in her mouth, creating the appearance of an odd toothy pout. She calmed down enough to correct the position of her dentures and looked at Pat expectantly. Pat smiled.

"Come on, really."

"OK, I'm not pregnant."

"MmmHmm?"

"I'm getting married."

Pat smiled again. "No, really, Nan."

"No, really, little girl. I am indeed getting married. Getting hitched. I am telling you I got myself another ball and chain."

"Get out!" Pat whooped and stood up to give her nan a big hug. "You old dog. How'd you meet him?"

"Bowling. His name is Buck and you can meet him at Sunday brunch after church, if you want."

"I want. I want." Pat settled back into her chair and they chatted for the rest of the afternoon. She had even persuaded Nan to open a second bottle of her homemade brew.

I can't believe Nan is getting married. Pat could hardly finish rereading her postcard. In fact, she could believe her nan was getting married. What she couldn't believe was that she herself had not had one date all year. Nan always accused her of being too picky. And maybe she was.

From the junk drawer, Pat retrieved an old snapshot of Sister Polly dangling from a swing. She smoothed the bent edges and decided to write again. On a whim, she'd sent herself the postcard before she'd left work for holidays. Now she felt like writing something more than just a greeting to herself.

"Who do I want?"

"Pat."

"I wasn't talking to you, Sister. Be quiet and let me think."

She tapped the table with her fingernail.

"Tok, tok, tok."

"Shh, Sister."

"Banana?"

"Shh!"

She held her pen tightly. Silence. She found herself thinking of a man. He was a customer who had come to the shop to order "Get Well" balloons for a friend. Pat wasn't sure why she remembered him at all. He was not remarkable. Tall, skinny, in his thirties with lank brown hair. But as he walked away, she noticed a limp that had not at first been apparent. He hadn't smiled at her until he paid for his balloon bouquet and was walking out the door. When he said "thanks again," it was like he was joking. When he smiled, it was like he was letting her in on the joke.

The pen, still clenched in Pat's hand, slipped uncomfortably as she moved it over the slick surface of the photograph.

☙ ❧

Nan called Pat an incurable perfectionist and perhaps that was true. Why else would she be at the strip mall checking in on the balloon shop the second day of her holiday?

Pat became her own boss thanks to a government program designed specifically to help young female entrepreneurs. She first applied for assistance to open a flower shop, but had been turned down due to the over-abundance of florists already operating in the town of Sherwood Park. Her loan officer told her that the program was specifically looking to back exciting and innovative young female entrepreneurs. Pat applied again, this time proposing a new way to send a birthday message or an I Love You on Mother's Day. High Flying Balloons was a creative alternative to flowers and was exciting and innovative enough to get her into the government program.

When she entered the store, her assistant was sitting at the counter reading *InStyle* magazine and twirling her frizzy hair into ringlets that stood from her head like antennae. Pat advanced and stood waiting at the counter. From this point of view, it was easy to see down Beth's gaping blouse. A black push-up bra accentuated her full breasts. As Pat shifted and coughed, Beth raised her head and leaned on the counter, further emphasizing her cleavage.

"How's the vacation treating you?" Beth smiled at her boss, unconcerned that she'd kept Pat waiting.

"Not bad after the initial panic wore off." Pat met Beth's blank look without surprise. Beth wasn't the hardest worker, she certainly wouldn't understand not being able to relax. Maybe it was for this reason that Pat liked Beth, even though sometimes the girl's laziness was a bit much. Pat instinctively moved behind the counter, knelt down and started to pick up some spare balloons, which were scattered over the floor. Beth crossed her legs prettily, to give Pat room.

"Doesn't seem like much of a holiday to me." Pat jerked her head up at the sound of a different, deeper voice. "Am I interrupting you?" It was him. The lanky-haired guy stared down at her.

"Nope." She stood up, dusting her hands off on her jeans. "My nan always says it's a bad day if you're on your knees and there is no man around." Beth gave a snort of surprised laughter and Pat felt heat rise to her cheeks. She clenched her jaw. She couldn't believe she'd said this.

The man raised his eyebrow. "Quite the philosophy."

"That's my nan, full of pearls of wisdom she can just pull from her hat on any occasion." Pat wished she would stop talking now. "How'd you know I was on vacation?" she said, opting for a quick, safe change of topic.

Beth jumped in. "He was here yesterday asking for stuff we didn't have. I said maybe if you were here you could help him, but that you were on vacation. He left his name and phone number in case you came in." Beth pulled out a crinkled paper from her work apron and handed it to Pat, who glanced at it quickly. Jonas Cleary.

"I was passing by and saw you were here. I know it's your vacation, but I'm hoping you can help me out," he said. "It's my daughter's sixth birthday and I wanted to bring a couple piñatas to her party. It's hard to find anything like that in this town and I work nights, so a trip to the city is a bit of a hassle."

Pat studied him while he talked. There was something lopsided about him. He was over six feet tall, almost painfully thin, and older than she had first thought. Laugh lines were etched deeply around his eyes and mouth. He still had all his hair, though, even if it was fine and greasy. He stood with his hands in his pockets. His right shoulder sloped towards the ground.

"Where do you work?" she asked him and then, biting her tongue, asked herself why she had asked him.

"I play bass in a jazz quartet. We have a regular gig at the Four Seasons out on the highway."

"Well, let's see if we can help you." Pat pulled out her supplier's catalogue. "When do you need it by?"

"I've still got some time. The party is next Saturday."

"There's nothing in the catalogue. I'll give them a call." She moved to the back room and strained to hear Beth and Jonas's conversation. All she could catch was Beth's soft laughter. She returned with an air of calm efficiency and told Jonas that he could come by next Thursday after three o'clock to pick up the piñatas. She watched him leave the store. His back seemed straighter as he walked. She wondered if she had imagined his limp.

Pat grabbed a pen and flyer from her store and went outside to sit in the fresh air. She fished in her purse for a stamp, which she licked and stuck on the corner of the flyer. A bench on the sidewalk of a strip mall hardly afforded the best outdoor experience, but it was sunny and warm, and she wouldn't be there for long. She just wanted to jot something down. She chewed the tip of the pen. *His club foot hits the pavement at an unhappy angle. I pace myself to his awkward steps. I don't want to catch up to him, pass him, like all the other people on the street.* Pat paused. She felt self-conscious and raised her head, half expecting to find someone watching her. Crowds of people moved on the sidewalks, filtering in and out of the busy mall. She noticed a woman in a wheelchair looking in her direction but soon realized that hers was a blank, uninterested stare. She sat alone, still. The constant shifting mass of people soon hid the woman from Pat's view.

Pat looked around again and saw that no one was paying her any heed. She bent her head to her work and wrote quickly.

◈ ◈

Two mornings later when she saw the blue flyer in her mailbox it seemed strange and unfamiliar. She could hardly remember what she'd written and eagerly looked at the text scribbled in haste across the page. She read it aloud. *I want to lure him into a dark corner, press him into a damp wall and feel his unbalance.* Her voice was awkward. The words didn't come easily. She folded the paper and added the flyer to her growing pile of postcards.

Feeling somehow satisfied, she went to visit her nan, sending off another postcard on the way. Nan greeted her at the door holding a large book of samples. "You're just in time." Today they were picking out wedding invitations.

As she entered the kitchen, she saw Buck sitting at the table with a bottle of homemade beer in his hand. When she met

Buck at bowling, Pat had been surprised by his youthful appearance. "Yep, that's right," Nan said. "He's a young 'un. At my age it's hard not to rob the cradle."

Buck had put his arm protectively around Nan and looked at Pat. "Once both people are past the age of eighty, I figure there are no more cradles to rob."

As Pat took a seat opposite the happy couple, Buck passed her a beer and her nan repeated, "You're just in time. We have it narrowed down to three choices." Nan flipped the pages to show the invitations to Pat, who immediately chose the simplest of the designs on sable-coloured paper.

Buck leaned back happily in his chair. "You picked my favourite."

Nan pretended to pout. "I liked this one better." She pointed to a brightly decorated card with the words "Better Late Than Never" scrawled across the front.

"I might have guessed." Pat raised her eyebrow at Buck, who laughed.

"Of course, you can have any invitation you want, Belle." The man rocked forward on his chair and folded his fiancée into his arms.

Pat could just see the top of Nan's white hair and the bottom of her chin. When Nan wriggled down a little in order to breathe, Pat saw a large smile on her mouth. She'd forgotten her grandmother's name was Belle. As she watched the old couple she tried to imagine them as young lovers, but preferred to see the wrinkles and grey hair. She wondered what it would be like to kiss a sagging breast or an ear filled with coarse wiry hair. She shook her head, Nan broke free from Buck's embrace and they all toasted the new invitations. "Better Late Than Never."

◖ ◗

She sits on wheels, as walking people pass. Her white sweatshirt is lumpy, fat haphazardly stuffed into fleece. Pat's eyes skimmed the text. It was morning again. The days were passing quickly now and instead of looking out her window, Pat sat with her coffee and stared at her postcard. She had picked it up in a junk store from a box of old photos and cards. It was from Spain. There was a flamenco dancer in the centre of the picture. Dark hair fanned out around her head as she twirled and her skirt was made of real material glued onto the cardboard. Pat touched the material. It was made of nylon, which snagged against her rough fingertips.

When she had worked in flower shops, her hands were perpetually dry. Stripping roses of their thorns tended to strip fingers of their skin. Now, the balloons hardly seemed better. Her nan suggested that it might be chemicals, slathered Pat's hands in Vaseline and secured white cotton gloves around her fingers.

Pat watched her fingers caress the postcard and wondered if she could show it to someone. It seemed a mystery, as if it had appeared in her life through no will of her own. She remembered seeing the woman in a wheelchair. She remembered thinking how calm the woman was even though she was forced into inaction by the milling crowd. She remembered desiring that calm. *She waits, and I think how patiently her fingers would move over my skin, how thoroughly she could pull pleasure from my throat.*

"Banana!"

Pat sighed and went into the sitting room to look in on Sister Polly. The bird lifted his feet excitedly one after the other in an eager dance.

"Pat. How are you?"

"I'm fine."

"How are you?" The parrot seized hold of his perch and spread his wings wide. He flapped noisily, banging his toy bell against the sides of his cage. The room filled with dust and small soft feathers. Pat grabbed her purse and headed out the door. She walked briskly down the street, deciding the short hike downtown would do her good. As she passed Nan's, she saw that both the screen door and storm door were shut tight. Two empty bottles of beer sat side by side on the stairs of the front porch. The railing was freshly painted a bright turquoise blue and the hedge was newly trimmed, but the house looked completely empty. It seemed Pat never could tell when her nan would be home now that she was engaged to Buck. Since she was so close to High Flying Balloons, she decided to drop in, thankful that she still knew what to expect from her store.

⊀ ⊁

On Saturday the mall was always busy and even her little shop had customers. She kept an eye open for Jonas Cleary, but didn't see him and chastised herself for wishful thinking. Looking into her crowded store for one brief second, Pat considered waiting and showing Beth her postcards. She fingered a card in her jacket pocket, fraying its edges with her fussing. It was one of those free postcards, which businesses print up as advertisements. Pat was thinking of doing some for her own store. This one was for a new sports shop specializing in snowboards, skateboards and mountain bikes. It was a store decidedly meant for the youth of the community. Every day, there seemed to be more and more shops like it popping up in the conservative downtown core of Sherwood Park. Pat liked these stores, even though she was too intimidated to walk inside them.

She had picked up the card in the entrance of a coffee shop. She liked the bright colours and, unlike most of its kind, it had enough space to actually write something on the back. On the front, there was a cartoon girl wearing a tuque and baggy pants. She had a beat-up old skateboard under her arm and a bubble over her head that communicated her thoughts: Girls Rule Boys Drool.

On the card, Pat had scribbled a quick message. *When I was a teenager.* It was becoming easier to write. These little notes seemed safe, even though she knew she ran the risk of exposure by mailing the postcards. She was reminded of the small red diary she had as a girl. It came with a lock and key and across the top of each page the date was etched in gilded letters. She'd kept the diary for five years, writing faithfully, but when the pages ran out Pat stopped writing. By that time she was too pre-occupied with school and friends and boys.

Pat read her most recent message about her first boyfriend, who had longish hair that curled over his shoulders and soft, full hips. Everyone mistook him for a girl. Pat liked him because he let her squeeze his pimples. *But he was young. My later partners weren't so enthusiastic and were, unfortunately, clear skinned.* Eventually, Pat broke up with him because he did not kiss well. When she told her nan this, the old woman chastised her, saying that anyone could be taught how to kiss.

Pat had a sudden urge to talk to Nan. She turned on her heel and headed for Nan's, where she found the old woman sitting on the porch shelling peas. Pat plunked down at her grandmother's feet and grabbed a handful of peas herself. She cracked the shells open and ran her thumb along the inside of the vegetable, dislocating peas in an efficient manner.

"I've been wanting to show you something." She read the card aloud.

Nan's voice was slow and slurred. "Must run in the family," she said. Pat leaned forward.

"I remember being pretty young, passing Kleenexes to my mom as she swabbed pus from a large boil on my dad's shoulder. I used to imagine Mom's hand stroking those raw red bumps on his back, but I never pictured them in the dark 'cause the care Mom gave Dad was always given in the brightest light." Nan hiccupped. "I guess she needed to see what she was doing." She hiccupped again. "Buck stopped by for a drink," she explained. Hiccup. "I need some water, dear."

Pat fetched a drink for Nan and concluded that perhaps she hadn't fully explained the situation, perhaps she had given a bad example, perhaps she would wait and try Nan again in the cooler air of the morning without the influence of beer.

Nan tilted the glass to her lips and downed the water. She took Pat's hand and said, "I feel better. Let's go get my dress." Pat nodded and put the card into her pocket.

They slowly walked the few blocks downtown to the street that had all the finer dress shops and stopped in the one bridal store of the town, joking about the various styles of wedding dresses, from Bo Peep to lemon meringue pie. As Nan tried on a beautiful flapper-style gown made of white silk and hundreds of beads, Pat listened to the woman in the next stall complain about her body. She was young, in her late twenties with soft brown hair. Pat closed her eyes and tried to picture her next postcard. Maybe something scenic. A waterfall. She saw the woman's stretch marks as the northern lights, a glorious pattern of stars sprayed across ginger skin. She imagined gliding her hand up razor-scraped thighs to trace the curve of the woman's waist and touch the side of her breast, finger stroking under arm.

Pat opened her eyes to Nan swirling in front of her, beads flying and shimmering in the sun, which streamed through the store window. "TaaaDaaa," Nan said, her arms spread wide, her face flushed with the movement.

They had the dress wrapped and went for lunch at a greasy diner where Nan like to get her tea leaves read. They ate their favourite, grilled cheese sandwiches, and split an order of fries. For dessert, they ordered a chocolate milkshake, which Nan sucked up through a straw while Pat spooned the extra into her mouth from a big metal container. Alma, the psychic, came by to say hi to Nan. She wore a long dress with jeans underneath. A small smear of ketchup stained the middle of her top. Dark hair covered her upper lip and the backs of her hands. She clasped Nan's hand in her own and said that she looked wonderful. Alma turned Nan's palm over and peered into it, her face brightened. "Good news. Happiness."

She took Pat's hand, studied her palm, patted her arm and said, "Don't worry, you have nothing to fear." Nan looked on approvingly, nodding her head in agreement.

◖◗

Pat stood in the line-up at the grocery store, flipping through the *TV Guide*. The woman in front of her was buying milk, broccoli, two plaid throw pillows and a small glass teapot, which when you removed the top half, became a cup. Pat wondered at buying such items from a food store. She followed the woman out of the store and watched her unlock her car. The woman was elderly, though not as old as her nan. She wore a yellow pantsuit of comfortable cotton fleece and drove a new, shiny green sedan. Pat felt a surge of envy. The woman's life seemed so secure. What would it be like to not wake up to a question every day? What was *normal*, anyway?

When she was a girl and people would tell her how pretty she was, their eyes held a promise—good things happened to good-looking girls. But "good things" seemed only to include meeting a handsome, young man and settling down. In school, all her friends talked about was how the teen star Shaun Cassidy was so dreamy or how Billy Broder in seventh grade was to die for. They'd dare Pat to go talk to him at lunch and she would. She didn't care about his blonde feathered hair and straight teeth, she had her eye on someone else. The boy in the back of the class with the slouch and the glasses.

One day she told her friends who she really liked. A chorus of "Ewww" rang out across the schoolyard. No one sat with her at lunch that day. "Cooties" was whispered just loud enough for Pat to hear. The next day, Pat told her friends she'd been joking. She'd learned what it meant to keep up appearances.

Now, when people tell Pat how pretty she is, there is nothing in their eyes but questions—what's wrong with you? why are still alone?

Pat watched the woman in the green pantsuit drive away and went home with her groceries. She ate lunch while reading about Dolly Parton's breast reduction surgery in a tabloid.

On the subscription card inside, Pat wrote her next postcard.

I have started to read the Enquirer and Weekly World News like dirty magazines. She described Lobster Man, Ape Man, man with two heads, eleven fingers, extra arm, missing torso. Cyclops. She wondered why it was always about an addition or subtraction, more or less from the average, the typical, the accepted, the oh-so-attractive. Pat flipped to an article about a vampire who sued his employers for a hundred thousand dollars because they wouldn't let him work in the dark. "Anton Khoroni says his rare condition makes it impossible for him to tolerate daylight . . ." She chewed her pen and decided that if she met Anton, she would tell him that the dark world is just as good as the light. *I would extinguish all fluorescence and would gain my sight by the radiance of his pale pure skin.* She continued. *But I don't buy these magazines for the articles; I buy them strictly for the pictures.* With cheap black ink from the newsprint smeared on her fingers, she touched herself.

◖◗

The sun was high in the sky and Sister Polly was chatting away in the other room. Pat drew all the blinds in the house tightly shut and went to sleep in an artificial night. She dreamt that she was herself, but she was also Dolly Parton. She was being interviewed by Barbara Walters. Her breasts seemed too large; they rubbed against her arms as she shifted in her seat. Her voice seemed too loud. She was trying to explain something. *People always say, "But you're not bad looking." Then I try to clarify that it is not my ugliness that draws me to the imperfect; it is purely their beauty.*

◖◗

The next morning, even before Pat awoke, she knew it was Thursday, the day Jonas Cleary was coming to the store to pick up his order. She stayed in bed a little longer than usual, lingered over her coffee and chatted with the mailman as she planted tulip bulbs in her flowerbed for next spring. She wondered briefly if he ever read her postcards while walking his long route. But if he had, he gave no hint, chattering on about the weather. She liked his braces, but when they were removed, she'd be faced with perfectly straight teeth. Perhaps it was enough that he seemed nice? Metal glinted in the sun when he smiled and handed Pat a bunch of envelopes before striding away down the sidewalk.

Only junk mail for her today. She ate a quiet lunch and played with Sister Polly in the afternoon. She did not think of Jonas. As the day darkened, her stomach clenched. Twilight was her least favourite time of day. Everything became indistinct. She had to strain her eyes to focus. She turned on all the lights in her house, even the overhead ones, which she usually found too harsh.

She took out a blank sheet of writing paper and looked forward to marking its whiteness. She liked the freedom of writing messily. She liked ignoring the rules she'd learned in grammar. Carefully placed commas, periods inside the end quotation mark, no run-on sentences. The last was a particular challenge for Pat, she loved running on.

When I have fear, my greatest is blindness. But when I imagine myself blind, I see attraction groping hands feeling space to move forward in shadow and then maybe my strange strangers would come to me because their fear would be freed by my sightless night and they would forget how sensitive my hands have become they would think that I would not know their deformity they would feel safe and I would feel their scars their twisted missing limbs their less than perfect shells and I would keep them safe in my shaded touch.

She put her pen down and rested her head in her hands. Not think of Jonas Cleary. He was probably still married anyway. But then wouldn't his wife be able to pick up the piñatas? And he did say he wanted to bring the piñatas to the party. That certainly sounded like he would be a guest at the party, not a daddy who's always home. Right? Not think of him.

This was the last day of her vacation. She'd wanted to take the weekend off, but every second Friday was when she placed her orders. Her mind was already on business again.

She went into Sister Polly's room and watched the bird

groom himself, obsessively picking the feathers from the right side of his neck. As Pat opened the cage, the parrot playfully bit at the latch and her fingers. Sister used his beak like fingers. The bird was so dexterous that metal clips had to be hooked through the bars to secure the food and water trays and the door of the cage. Once free, Sister Polly lost no time finding his way to Pat's shoulder.

"Give me a kiss," Pat said, turning her lips towards the bird.

Sister replied with a quick peck of a curved beak to Pat's mouth.

"Let's sit down. My holiday is almost over and you didn't even get any loving." As she sat with her legs up, the parrot ducked his head under Pat's chin. She lifted her hand to stroke Sister's head. She grimaced as she noticed how dirty the cage was. Seeds and shit covered the bottom. Delicate white feathers stuck to old banana caked on the bars of the bird's house. "I've been neglectful," she explained to Sister, who didn't respond, but rolled his eyes back with the pure bliss of being caressed. Pat smiled at the parrot and moved her fingers down to stroke Sister's neck. Underneath the bird's feathers, Pat could feel Sister's tiny fragile skeleton. She pressed her thumb and forefinger around the parrot's vulnerable throat.

"Banana." The parrot's loud voice was especially piercing when spoken directly into Pat's ear.

Pat sighed, rose from the couch and walked into the kitchen with the bird. "Here we go. A yummy banana." Sister Polly took the fruit and ate it in delicate bites while Pat stared out her window. She opened the window for fresh air and quickly retreated to the other room before Sister had time to realize just how close freedom lay.

◄◎ ◎►

She saw a woman jogging towards her on the street. Pat quickened her step and squinted into the distance to get a better look. The woman wore shiny nylon running shorts and had her socks pulled high on her calves. There was nothing remarkable about her except an odd shape around her middle. Pat squinted more. What was that shape? A growth, maybe? A malformation? The jogger passed Pat, who paused to sit on a bench by the tennis courts. Her knees felt a little weak, her forehead damp. She could hear the *thwupp* of rackets hitting balls and she shook her head. The woman was only wearing a fanny pack tucked under her shirt. Nothing to get excited about. Just calm down. It was eight in the morning, Friday. Pat continued through the park to her shop. Her vacation was over.

She opened the store's door and switched on the lights. Usually, she came in early to do some arrangements before having to deal with the public. Today, especially, there would be extra work to do since Beth had been left alone for almost two weeks. Pat sat at the counter sipping her coffee and looked at the postcard in front of her. She had wanted something fun, something different. Yesterday, she finally mustered her courage and walked into the snowboard shop. Inside, no one noticed her as she slowly spun the card rack around so that she could study all of her possibilities. She stopped when she found the one she wanted.

The card in front of her had a seventies guy on it, striking a disco pose on a floor alight with colours—red, pink, yellow, green. His one finger pointed up and his other finger pointed down. His eyes were half closed and his mouth was open. He had a big brown Afro and wore his shirt open to the waist. His pants were made of silver, which matched the word written across the bottom in shiny 3D characters. FUNKY. She flipped the card. On the back, there was a miniature of the disco guy and written beside him in bold black letters was **Hey, call me Randy!**

Pat looked around her store and sighed. She didn't know what to write. She looked at her window display filled with orange and brown balloons to represent the coming fall season. She sighed. Her glance rested on the shelves filled with balloons and cups and teddy bears and little angel statuettes. She looked at her own Gemini coffee mug and the yellow Post-it notepads that she had in two sizes, small and smaller. Sighed. Suddenly, she heard a tapping at the shop door. She grabbed the blank card, hastily wrote some words on the back and shoved it in her purse.

Moving towards the storefront, she unlocked the entrance. Jonas Cleary stood in front of her with a sheepish look on his face. "I know you're not open yet, but I saw you through the window." Pat nodded and kept the door close to her. He continued, "I didn't get a chance to stop by for those piñatas and the party is tomorrow. I haven't even got home to sleep yet." He looked expectantly into the store.

"Sure. Come on in." She moved to the back and grabbed his order, ripping off a note Beth had left with a big question mark written on it.

"Great. Thanks. I really appreciate it. Now my wife can only be pissed at me for not coming home last night."

Pat nodded, took his money and handed him a receipt. She walked him to the door, planning to lock it again since she had another good hour before officially opening. Suddenly, he turned back and she bumped into him. His leg connected with hers and she marvelled at the solid, hard contact of his knee. He staggered a little and again she noticed the stiff movement of his right side. He looked down, rubbed his upper leg and shrugged. When he said "Thanks again," it was like he was joking. When he smiled, it was like he was letting her in on the joke.

She closed the door. Closed her eyes.

He sits heavily on the side of her bed, sheds his shirt, takes off his pants and removes his fake leg. He asks if she minds. He explains it is more comfortable sleeping without it. Even though he speaks bluntly, she hears tension in his voice. He would rather not reveal himself but has grown accustomed to issuing the challenge. She undresses and climbs into bed. He curls his back into and against her heat. As she falls asleep with her hand soft around the curve of his absent leg, she smiles and thinks exactly just how much she does not mind.

The day dragged. Summer was a slow time for a balloon store. Pat sketched out some designs for Nan's wedding. Her grandmother wanted Pat to decorate the hall and make a special arrangement of balloons for the bridal bouquet. Pat dawdled over her work, feeling uninspired. She closed shop fifteen minutes early and went directly home. The kids playing hockey in the street accidentally sent a ball flying her way, which hit her bare leg with a loud slapping noise. She shrugged off their apologies and entered her house with a stinging round red spot on her shin. Her eyes watered. She tossed her bag on a chair. It slid off and its contents scattered to the floor. Lipstick rolled under the fridge, change clattered across the tiles and the **Hey, call me Randy!** card slid under the table. As she was bending down to retrieve it, a loud voice sounded in the kitchen.

"Banana!"

Pat jumped, bumping her head on the edge of the table. She looked around her and saw Sister Polly sitting above the sink, on the ledge, in front of the open window. Pat realized she must have forgotten the second latch the last time she'd put Sister back in the cage. The window made a perfect frame for the parrot, who was perched directly in the middle and was backdropped by the green weeping willows that lined the street outside. The wind stirred, blowing the delicate leaves of the trees and ruffling Sister's feathers.

"Pat?"

"Yes, Sister Polly, it's Pat. How are you?" Pat fell into the regular routine while slowly approaching the bird.

"How are you?" Sister replied.

"I'm fine." Pat was around the table, now edging toward the window. The wind stirred again and the parrot spread its wings. Sunlight illuminated each soft grey feather and then the bird took flight. There was a storm of dust and pinfeathers. Pat blinked once and then Sister landed on her shoulder.

"Banana!" Sister insisted and Pat laughed, sinking to the floor in relief. She stroked the bird's head and felt happy when its claws dug into her flesh as Sister dipped down to better receive Pat's caresses.

Beside her, her bag lay empty. It looked deflated. Change was scattered everywhere. Keeping one hand on the bird, Pat moved her foot to shake off the nickels and dimes, which stuck to her sweaty skin. As she bent her leg, the postcard slid out from under the table. Pat read her last message to herself. Her name was printed neatly in the space under the stamp, but the writing was a messy scrawl covering the whole back of the card.

I'm not sure when I first realized my desire for imperfection. I think it was even before I realized desire.

Pat stood up, closed the window and put the bird back in its cage.

Close to Home

My dad gathers me in a brief, bone-crushing bear hug and doesn't stop talking during the entire car ride from the airport to the city. He has more grey hair and stoops slightly but otherwise looks the same. His skin is tanned a deep brown, even though he hasn't worked a construction job in a few years. His eyebrows are unruly. The laugh lines at the corners of his eyes almost join his dimples, forming two perfect half moons of wrinkles around his face. He has developed a new habit of sucking at his teeth in between sentences, a loud smacking sound like he's trying to taste something at the back of his mouth. "Dentures," he explains when he sees my gaze trained on his lips.

It's hard to think of my dad as a senior citizen. He's ten years older than my mom and they married quite late for their generation. "Had to get hitched," my mom laughs when she talks about their wedding. "I had a bun in the oven, as they say, and I was already twenty-five, wasn't getting any younger."

But despite the wrinkles, my dad seems youthful. His arms are still muscled and he smoothly changes gears as we stop for a yellow light. He continues his commentary on Edmonton's development. *Dead-monton,* my friends and I called it as teenagers. "That over there, remember? Was a gas station. Now, it's a pizza place. Thin crust." I watch the scenery pass and have the strange sensation that everything is exactly the same as when I left, even though I see evidence of both change and decay. I don't care about the buildings. It is the sky that feels like home. A big blue prairie sky that covers my eyes like a blindfold.

It's been three years since I moved away and this is my first trip back. After high school, not really knowing what to do, I found a job in the main commissary for Smitty's Restaurant. My shift started at five in the morning and I spent the day making pies. My workstation was next to the deep fryer. No matter how much I washed my hair, the smell of egg rolls remained. The other woman "on pies" had been doing the same job for a decade. She probably wasn't even forty, but her hair was thinning and her shoulders sagged. I'd been working there a couple of years already when one day she looked at me across the lunch table and drew a long drag off her cigarette. "Karen," she said, squinting through smoke. "You remind me of someone."

"Who?" I asked between bites of strawberry cream pie.

She pointed a yellowed finger to her own sunken, bony chest and stared at me.

I lowered my fork to my plate and tasted sugar on my lips as I tried to smile. The next day I started to research universities. Many of my friends had already left Edmonton, most going west to Vancouver. I decided to go east and was twenty-three when I moved to Montreal to attend Concordia. When I left home, I was sure I would visit every year, twice a year even, but summer turned to fall to winter to spring. The school thing didn't last long. Papers and exams bored me as much as pies. I found a job and then the timing for travel never seemed right. Until now.

Today, I need to be here in the car with my dad and the sky. We cross the river and pass through the small city centre. Dad speeds up over a little hill, and my stomach rises and falls as the truck tips up and then dips down. He used to do this for my sister and me when we were girls. I'd squeal with nervous laughter and Libby, though four years older, would bury her head in my lap. Now I feel a slight pull where my stitches were. The doctor said the incision was healing nicely. Maybe I'm imagining the pain?

We pass over railroad tracks and I lift my feet. We turn onto a street that cuts through a graveyard and I hold my breath. When we cross into the west side of town, I sit up a little straighter, waiting to round a bend in the road that will reveal the house I was born in. "Gone," Dad says, avoiding my eyes. A second later I understand. A shiny new strip mall covers the block where our old house once stood.

"Prime real estate," Dad explains. "Mrs. Walker died a couple years ago. She pretty much owned the whole street, so with her gone it went up for sale."

"Why didn't Mom tell me?" Since moving to Montreal the phone has been my only connection to my family. I know I should call more often, but whenever I do my dad answers, mumbles a brief "how are you" and passes me to my mom, who tells me all about what the neighbours have planted in their garden and how much it rained last night.

Dad shrugs, "Didn't want to upset you."

I clamp my mouth shut. I need this visit to be good. Almost two months since I had the operation and no one would know to look at me, but I'm tired. I let my head lean against the window and try to picture the house I grew up in.

Mrs. Walker was my parents' landlady for twenty-one years. Libby and I called her place the gingerbread house because it had a tall, peaked roof and was covered in decorative white lattice that looked like frosting. Our family rented the small house next door. It had a red roof and a huge backyard, which was lined with plum trees that would blossom full of pink flowers in the spring and drop squishy ripe fruit all summer long.

My parents first moved there when my sister was born. They paid a hundred and twenty-five dollars a month for two small bedrooms, a kitchen and a living room. There was no basement. When my baba came to live with us before going into a nursing home, she never could unpack her suitcase because there was no extra closet space. "Cozy," she said, her thick Ukrainian accent making the word sound like an order.

Her bed was across from the bunks Libby and I shared. She smelled like garlic and snored, but my sister and I were happy to have her close by. She made us pies from Saskatoon berries and let us dip rhubarb from the garden into a bag of brown sugar.

In the summer, the small size of the house didn't matter. Libby and I were always outside with friends. One girl, Penny Little, used to lift her pretty pink dress and pee beside our plum trees until our baba caught her and sent her away. My favourite place to play was the nearby ravine. The older kids would tell scary stories of the witch who lived down in the river valley and boiled children in her brew. A tree house stood in the quiet, cool pines. Brown needles poked my bare feet. When we played hide and seek, the tree house was the safe place you had to get back to. I'd conceal myself in the little forest and watch until the coast was clear, then I'd run as fast as I could, always relieved when I arrived and was able to cry out, "Home!"

I was seventeen when we moved. My parents were happy to finally become homeowners and I was excited to have a room of my own, but I still cried when we left. After the move, I'd sometimes pass by our old place and each time there was something different. A fence was built, the swing set rusted, the weeping willow was cut back and the garden sodded. Only the plum trees remained the same, and I would walk the edge of the boulevard and suck the sweet fruit from its skin and feel good. But now where the plums trees stood, there's a paved alley where employees park and put out garbage.

Dad has stopped talking and we travel into the suburbs to my parents' house in silence.

As the truck rolls into the driveway, my mom opens the back door, and a small fluffy dog runs out and barks at me. "Gizzy! Gizzy, stop that. Come back here." Mom moves towards me, but I'm too busy trying to fend off the mutt, which is now bouncing off my legs.

Dad joins in the chorus of admonitions. "Gizzy, that's enough." But both my parents are laughing. I was surprised when they told me they got a dog. Growing up, I begged for a pet. One year, I even made a calendar called *Six Weeks to Waiting for a Puppy* because I was convinced that this would be the Christmas my dream would come true. Instead, I got a record player, a bunch of Play-Along 45s and two stuffed animals. "They don't need to be walked," my mom said cheerfully.

"I can't believe it." I bend down and pick up the squirming animal.

Mom hugs me loosely so as not to crush Gizzy, who licks

her face when she comes close. She laughs again. "Yes, you love Nana, don't you?" She reaches for the dog and I get a good look at my mom. For this occasion, she has changed from her usual sleeveless flowered housedresses into a beige blouse and brown slacks. She's gained a little weight but looks healthy. Her hair is cut short and permed curly. As we walk to the house, she favours her right leg and I see a gauzy bandage peeking out from her sandals. She wears darkened glasses because her eyes are sensitive from the laser surgery.

She's been a diabetic since I was born, shooting insulin into her thigh every morning and avoiding sugar except during a reaction, when sweat pours from her brow as she sits down, eats three chocolate bars and spoons honey into her mouth. The doctors tell her she's been lucky, even though she has sores on her feet that won't heal, and her eyes are bleeding.

"That's what I'm scared of most—going blind," she'd say, and even as a child I could feel the terror in her voice and her fear became mine. When I was ten, I was convinced I was losing my sight because we had to change my eyeglass prescription twice in one year. I stayed home curled on the couch, watching soap operas and faking sick, a rosary clutched in my hand, praying. A large round bead, *Our Father who art in heaven*—please don't let me go blind—ten Hail Marys—oh please God, don't let me go blind. My mom slowly climbs the steps to the back door. Please God don't . . .

The house smells like pine cones. An electric freshener in the shape of a Christmas tree is plugged into the wall by my feet. It's cold inside. "Close the door, honey, we've got the air on. I tell you, I complained when your dad put it in. I thought it was going to be another white elephant, as they say. Like that huge Rototiller he got for a bargain." Mom draws out the last word and mimes quotation marks in the air to stress her sarcasm. "It was really great a couple of summers ago when I had the sweats all the time. I thought the change was supposed to be hot then cold, but I was just hot, then hot, then hot again."

I forget sometimes that my mom is so much younger than my dad. She can still remember getting cramps with her periods and scrubbing blood stains from panties. Is this why I haven't told her? Because it's still close enough for her to fully imagine? Just a routine check-up. I didn't give it another thought—until I got the call a month later. Results abnormal.

"How's your eye?" I change the subject.

"Oh God, the stupid doctors. If I never saw another one it'd be too soon. I hate them. I hate the doctors."

I nod. "Is Libby out of town?"

"She's in Hinton for the week doing one of her training sessions at the hospital. Showing the other nurses some new procedures or something."

"Where's dad?"

"Probably smoking in the garage."

My dad calls the garage his "office." The walls are lined with tools. Most of them aren't used anymore. My mom argues it should be cleaned out. "He's got six hammers," she told me on the phone. "Who needs six hammers?"

"They're all different," I could hear my dad's voice in the background.

I clear my bags from the entry, splash some water on my face and go outside to consult with my dad in his office. We drink Pilsner. He sits in a plastic chair, leaning forward, resting his elbows on his knees. He's wearing slippers and I suddenly wonder if he had them on at the airport. "They found brother Bill," he says.

This is news. My uncle Bill is the family mystery. What ever happened to Uncle Bill? He packed a bag and disappeared from the farm as a young man. No one in the family has heard from him since.

"How'd they find him?"

"Dead. The RCMP phoned Auntie Helga and asked her if she had a brother Bill. Apparently, he'd been living with a woman in a rooming house in Toronto. She found his identification and all the names and phone numbers of our family.

That's the damnedest thing. He had all our current numbers just like he'd been calling us for years."

When I was young I used to wonder about Uncle Bill. What would it be like to leave your family? I always imagined a helium balloon cut loose to float in the air. A fast escape, a dance on the wind, but it wouldn't be long before it sailed far away and disappeared from sight completely. I'd run to my mom and sit in her lap. She'd twirl her finger in my long hair and hold on.

"Did you find out why he left?"

"No. Probably never will." Dad slides his slippered feet across the garage floor. "Want another one?" He takes two cans from a cooler and pops the tops. The screen door of the house squeaks open and bangs shut. Dad and I join Mom on the patio.

I stretch and turn my face to the warmth of the day. "Am I ever happy to be on holidays," I say, feeling slightly self-conscious in my attempt to make small talk.

Mom responds easily, "I was surprised you got to take off in the summer. Isn't it your busy season?"

My throat tightens. I never thought my mom would question the timing of my visit. She takes off her glasses to look at me. I study the ground. It'd be so easy to say, "Sick leave."

My hands cradle my stomach. "Seniority," I say, and ramble on. "It was crazy busy when I left, what with the tourists on the road and the highway stays warm till late at night. The deer come out of the woods for the heat. We've got a skunk problem, too." Now my dad's also looking at me and I stop talking. I realized early on that nobody wanted to hear about my job and my parents are no exception. Hell, I don't even want to hear about my job. But it's not as bad as people think.

After spending a year in university, studying nothing in particular, I looked forward to the summer and a chance to work and make some money. I found a job with the Ministère des Transports du Québec and pictured sunny days of cutting grass by the highway or holding a *SLOW* sign to direct traffic around road construction. When it turned out I was on road kill duty, I was slightly disturbed, to say the least. As a little girl riding in my parents' car, I used to cross myself three times when I saw a dead dog or cat or porcupine on the highway. I'd squeeze my eyes tight and pray there was an animal heaven.

But the job wasn't that bad. I didn't have to speak French. I got used to working nights and, after my week's training period, I was let loose alone on the highway. This was close enough to my childhood ambition to be satisfying. I'd always wanted to drive the big rigs. While other girls played teacher, I played truck stop. My mom told me that if I cried as a baby, my dad would take me for a spin around the block, and I'd be gurgling happily by the time the ride was over. I'm most content when I'm going somewhere, even if the destination is a dead deer.

The summer job turned permanent when one of the full-time staff took early retirement. The funny thing was my parents didn't seem to mind me dropping out of school. I always thought they wanted something better than blue collar for their kids. But they did get to tell people I worked for the government and I got the impression they were just thankful I'd settled down into something.

"Joe called, he was wondering when you got in," mom says brightly. "He's got some tickets to the Folk Festival." She feeds bits of her sandwich to the dog and I get up to phone my first love.

◀◎ ◎▶

When I leave the house that evening, I'm powdered, perfumed and pepperminty fresh. I have even optimistically shaved my legs all the way up to my crotch. I'm going to meet Joe. Big Joe, The Joker, Little Joey or Pickles, as he likes to be called. I'm driving my mom's sedan. I've found an old tape of the Cure in the basement, which I pop into the stereo. *The very first time I touched your skin I thought of a story and watched it reach the end too soon.*

As I drive the twisting road into the river valley, I squirm in my seat. I feel sexy. I feel sixteen. The cool evening air streams in through my open window and I taste the sweet smell of dried grass. The streets are full of cars. I park on a gravel side road, walk back a few blocks and cross a small footbridge to get to the ski club. The stages are set up on the small bunny hills and there are crowds of people milling about, but I quickly spot Joe at the entrance gates and skip up to meet him. He picks me off the ground and twirls me around in an oh-so-happy embrace. We link arms and go to the beer gardens, where we sit on the ground and tell each other how good we look.

Joe is a handsome man. He's a big man. "I'm a fat man," he says, laughing. "Actually, the boys are going to kick me out of the fat club soon, if I don't gain a bit more weight. That's the problem with this job, it's too healthy." He lifts his plastic Labatt's cup and toasts the air. "And I don't get to drink nearly enough beer." This summer, he's been painting houses as opposed to the bartending jobs he's had since high school. He's lost that pasty look bar people get from too much free liquor and never seeing the sun. But he's always been shy about compliments. "My eyebrows are going bald," he says when I tell him his lips are beautiful.

I ask him what else he's been up to. He responds, "I'm writing a short story."

"Really?"

"Yeah. It's about my penis."

I groan. He asks about my family. "They're fine. You know. Same." I answer vaguely because I don't really know yet. "How's yours?"

"Crazy. They're nuts! We all are. It's a good thing we're a family because nobody else could stand us. Sally slept with Jean-Claude Van Damme. She was working as a chambermaid in a hotel and the next thing you know . . ." This far north, on summer nights, light loiters in the sky. The sun escapes a cloud and silver shines at Joe's temples. "He's a Face Man, by the way. Picture that." Joe's sister has a list of categories to classify men sexually. The Face Man goes down on you, the Over Achiever is everywhere at once, but never gets you anywhere, The Wham-Bam-Thank-You-Ma'am is self-explanatory, and then there is The Keeper.

"But was he a Keeper?" Occasionally, the classifications can overlap. Obviously, only the Face Man can also be a Keeper, but there is that rare instance that a Keeper isn't a Face Man.

"She said 'yes.' Go figure."

"What's Sally doing now?"

"Mostly black men."

I mock hit him. He grins and we laze on the grass, falling into a comfortable silence. I'm glowing a little just being around him and I'm thinking this town's not so bad. Joe was my best romance. We met when we were sixteen and spent hours parked in his truck, pressing bodies, never naked, grinding hip to hip, groin to groin. When we felt queasy from so much chaste passion, we'd stare at the stars and wish dreams for each other.

In Montreal, I go through lovers like peanuts. "How's that guy you're seeing?" my mom asks whenever I phone. "Perry? Gary?"

"It's over with Gary, but I've met someone new."

"Another one?" her voice incredulous.

"Only one," I think, as the day disappears and I stroke Joe's thigh. His breath is damp and hot against my hair. I know he's smiling. A couple of girls come over. They're both tiny and cute and wear cowboy hats. They hand us a joint and I take a small puff, barely inhaling. We go sit with the crowds on the hill by the main stage and I feel roots growing from me, spreading into the ground, spreading, growing, from me into the ground. And I'm thinking those cowgirls have some wicked pot.

I spend the next three days at the festival with Joe and Penny Little, my childhood friend who used to pee in the garden. She's now married and has two kids. Even after my family moved and I switched high schools, we kept in touch. Her husband has taken their toddlers camping for the weekend. "I'm free," she says, as she gulps back beer and dances in front of the stages with her hands in the air. When she lifts her arms, her

T-shirt rides up and I can see the soft roll of her belly. I look at my stomach, perfectly flat except for a narrow, raised line, an incision that is hidden from everyone, including myself.

While the festival is on, I hardly see my parents. Instead, I see Alejandro Escovedo five times, once on the main stage and four times in the smaller workshops with other musicians. He steals my heart the first night when he sings a cover of "I Wanna Be Your Dog." *Now I'm ready to close my eyes. Now I'm ready to take your hand.* Distortion. The folkies don't know what hit them, but I love it. I am not often a fan, but when I become one, I'm dedicated. He starts to recognize me in the small crowds. He has dusky skin, wears dark wrap-around sunglasses, dresses in black, and has a sad smile that invites thoughts of salty necks, moist skin and open-eyed ecstasy. I can't help but wet my lips. On the final day, he says hi and I respond, "You're so great, I hope you never die."

The festival over, Joe goes back to work, complaining about the early mornings and long days. He promises to see me on the weekend. Penny invites me to visit her. "You have to meet my kids. Eva was just a baby when you left and Arlo wasn't even born yet. It's nice to have a break, but I miss them. I know every mom thinks this, but they really *are* amazing."

Promises are made to call each other, but my mind is already searching for excuses. I briefly think about telling her everything but quickly reject the idea. If I talk about it, I'll have to think about it and I'm not prepared to do that yet. It's like I've whitewashed my memory. And right now I'm protective of this blank wall, even though I know eventually the thin veneer will chip and fall away. When Penny and I say our goodbyes I avoid her eyes.

With my sister still out of town I'm left with nothing to do but pass days in the suburbs with my parents. I slow down and easily blend into their retired life. I drive my mom to her doctors' appointments at the foot clinic, the optometrist, the eye surgeon. I feel something has been accomplished when, in an afternoon, my dad and I get groceries at IGA where the lunch meat is good *and* go to Safeway where we have a dollar-off coupon for two litres of milk.

Mom's on the phone with Libby when we return, talking about her new vacuum cleaner. "It's a Phantom Fury. You should see all the gunk we got from the rug. It's gross!" she says, with enthusiasm. "Yeah, she's right here." The plastic of the receiver is warm against my ear.

Libby's voice is like my own. We speak in soft tones that can be easily drowned out, especially by the sound of running water. "I'll be back home on the weekend. Are you coming to the cat party?" she asks.

My sister self-admittedly wants to be one of those crazy old cat ladies. And by her estimate, she's well on her way. She's bought a ninety-two-year-old three-storey house on the north side of Edmonton where she lives alone, and she's adopted four cats so far. Ginger and Buddy came first. Buddy died a year later of feline leukemia. Libby grieved like a mother. After a time, Mom and Dad became worried and gave her Sebastian to try to break the depression. It helped some and Tookie helped some more. She found Tookie in a pet store with a sign on her cage saying, *Please take me home, I die tomorrow.* There was no question in Libby's mind. Every year Libby has a party to celebrate their adoptions.

I make sure I inquire about the cats.

"I'm a little worried," Libby responds. "My neighbour's been feeding them while I'm away and she says Ginger-cat's not eating her soft food. When I get back I'll go get her some baby beef liver. That might spark her appetite."

"I'm sure Ginger's fine," I say distractedly. My mom is watching daytime television, the volume on high. People bicker over small claims in a courtroom and everyone, including the judge, looks guilty.

Libby coughs into the phone. "Sorry," I tell her.

"It's OK. I've got to get back to work anyway."

We hang up and I feel bad. I wanted to tell her how much I'm looking forward to seeing her. My sister is smart and gentle and generous, but she's never had a boyfriend. When she's not at work she stays at home nestled into the couch under layers of homemade blankets and sleeping cats. The thought of her being lonely makes my heart squeeze into a protective fist.

My parents seem resigned to Libby's and my lack of success in relationships and they've never pressured us about having kids. Instead, they talk baby-talk to the dog. Much of their day is spent wondering if Gizzy is hungry, does she have to pee, is she bored?

I watch my parents in fascination. I want to scream, "It's a dog!" But I let them go on, thinking it's good they have something to discuss. Recently, in the car on the way to a doctor's appointment, my mom told me that sometimes she and dad could go days without saying a word to each other. She was talking about how a relationship can go through all sorts of phases in thirty years but the hardest part is making it through the dull times. I believe she was trying to make a point about my habit of dumping boyfriends. My mom's not the kind of person to sit me down and say, "Karen, you're twenty-six years old now, don't you think it's about time you settled down," but she does make her views known in other ways. Her admission about how she and Dad barely talk has not left me thinking about trying to hang in there with someone. Instead, I picture nights at my parents' house, my mom and dad eating supper together, the hum of air-conditioning the only sound to break the silence.

I head out to the garage for a smoke. I've started again. My guilt compounded even though cervical cancer is not linked to smoking. When the doctor called with the result of my pap test, she said that it was not "benign." I repeated this word in my head and pictured a cow languidly chewing cud. When I imagined cancer, I saw a scorpion curled in my belly, waiting to extend, waiting to sting.

"Fast-growing," the doctor said. Three days later I was in an operating room, hoping that when I woke up I'd still have my reproductive system. The anaesthetist told me to count to ten. A flash of pure panic. Then I heard someone saying, *ten, nine, eight* and the sky-blue ceiling faded to black. I don't remember closing my eyes.

I light another cigarette and my dad joins me for what has become our ritual late-afternoon beer. He tells me about his first job in a metal shop, where he worked for eighteen dollars a week and lived in a room with no kitchen, no toilet. Just a bed. From there, he travelled across Canada and the States. He squints, trying to put memories into focus. "Eventually, I got a job with the railroad. Had a gas station with brother Horst for a while at the same time, but it didn't last." Dad smiles shyly. "We went under. We had a good go of it for a bit when they were working on the highway. All the big trucks would stop. Even had a girl working for us in the coffee shop, but after the highway was repaired we realized we were on the wrong side of the road. Didn't get the traffic."

It's strange for me to imagine my father as a young wanderer. He'd stopped travelling and taking chances on risky business ventures by the time I was born. I do remember his job in the railroad yards. He started his shift at midnight, leaving the house in the dark with a thermos full of coffee and his metal lunchbox. Libby and I always wanted to make sandwiches for him. The next morning we would ask, "Did you like the sandwiches? We made them with two cheeses. Did you like the cookies?"

During the winter, we were especially concerned with providing treats for him. Even though I was supposed to be asleep, I often woke up to hear my dad quietly rustling in the kitchen, the soft light filtering through the half-closed door. I always felt bad that he had to leave our warm house while I stayed snug in my bed. Initially, he'd started working nights so he could look after us during the day while my mom went to her job. When we began school, Dad was able to quit the railroad and work construction. Sometimes, on weekends, he'd take us to a job with him. He'd tie a white carpenter's apron around our waists and start rows of nails for us to finish pounding in. I loved the efficiency of the heavy hammer in my small hands even though it would sometimes take me six tries to drive a nail home. My dad had it down to a consistent, rhythmic two swings—tock TOCK, tock TOCK, tock TOCK.

We hear the back door close and Mom comes into the garage. She folds her arms across her chest and rocks side to side, shifting weight, swaying. I have this same habit.

She joins the conversation, ticking jobs off on her fingers. "Dollar Cleaners. Phone operator. File clerk for the university farm. Waitress—which was a nightmare, as they say."

"When'd you start work for Woodward's?" I want her to keep talking. I realize this is why I've come back, this is where I come from, this is who I am.

When I found out I had cancer, I hung up my phone and stared. The cord swung slow circles, rhythmically tapping against the table leg, measuring out time. I wanted to call someone. The first person who came to mind was my mom. When I was young and hurt myself, I wouldn't run to my dad or baba or Libby, even though I knew they'd be good for sympathy. I'd look for my mom—in the garden, in the kitchen—I'd search everywhere until I found her, and when I did, she'd take me onto her lap, put her chin on my head and sigh a soft *shhh*. That one exhalation, her warm breath tickling my hair, and suddenly I was calm.

But my mom had just had surgery herself and Libby was always talking about how stress hindered the recuperation process. I did actually dial Libby's number, thinking that as a nurse she might be the perfect person to talk to, but when I got her machine I hung up and stared at the phone some more. I had friends in Montreal, the guys from work, two girls I knew from university, ex-lovers who'd remained friendly. But to call them and say, "I have cancer. I need surgery. I might not be able to have children." Well.

I picked up the phone and dialed. "Ministère des Transports du Québec, comment puis-je vous aider?" My boss understood completely, not to worry, they could easily find someone to replace me until I recovered.

As I listen to my mom, I feel greedy. Give me all the small

details of life. Her voice pours into a void I wasn't even aware existed. "I started work again just after you were born. The girls from the flower shop and I still laugh about that job when we get together." She looks at my dad and asks, "Remember the time I almost lost my job?"

It's hard to picture my mom being fired. A woman who is so responsible and organized that she calls me long distance to remind me to set my clock back in the fall and sends me stamps just in case I can't get to the post office.

Mom and Dad share smiles. She turns to me and explains, "There was this real fancy type in the garden centre. She was all done up. Her hair teased to high heaven. I was watering the plants and she kept standing in the way, so I asked her to move, but she stayed where she was—real bitchy-like. I turned around to get the roses in the corner and for some reason I thought she'd moved, so I turned back to water the plants I'd missed. But she was right behind me and the next thing I know she's dripping with ice-cold water and hollering bloody murder, as they say. Her hair came down off her head like an avalanche." Mom laughs while she tells her story, and her voice becomes louder and excited. Dad and I laugh, too. We laugh and laugh.

Mom gleefully pinches her nose. We fall silent, each of us looking at our own feet. Inside the house, the phone rings. Mom gets up and hurries to the door. I hear her distant "Hello," and then she's back. "It's Penny," she says.

Before I reach the phone, I have my excuse ready, "Hey Penny," I answer, striving for a light tone. Mom sits across from me, flipping through the *TV Guide*. "I would like to meet the kids, but I sort of planned on spending the evening with my parents." Mom looks up, flicks her hand and mouths, *Go ahead*. I shake my head and keep talking. "Yeah, I don't get to see them much. Maybe. OK. Bye."

"You should have gone," my mom says as she reaches for the remote. "Your dad and I were just going to watch the boob tube."

Dad comes in and sits down. "Going over to Penny's?" he asks.

"Don't feel like it," I say, and that is the truth, but I still feel dishonest. I just want this conversation to end. "What's on TV?"

Mom switches the channel to *Unsolved Mysteries*. Dad leans forward in his chair. "This is a good one," he says. But the true crime programs depress me. Men murdering children. Women murdering children. Children murdering children. I read my book instead. *High Fidelity* by Nick Hornby. The narrator, a sarcastic slacker type, has a habit of listing things: *I was going to ask you for your top five records to play on a wet Monday morning and all that, and now you've gone and ruined it.* It's a game not to be spoiled.

I, too, start to think in top fives. Top five liquor stores in Alberta: *The Booze Barn* and *Liquor Select* come in top two. The first advertises *Really, Really, Really Cold Beer* while the latter promises *Extremely Cold Beer*. *On 111th* is conveniently located on 111th Avenue. Then there is the ever-popular *Liquor Store*, of which there are hundreds. And finally, the *One Stop Shop*, a favourite because of their senior citizens' specials. Thursday, my dad and I go there for a 5 per cent discount on Pilsner. The errand takes us thirty minutes. We return to the house satisfied.

The house my parents bought when we moved from our small rental was never really home to me. It was bigger, stucco with green trim, but it lacked that warm, chicken-noodle, baked-bread feeling. And my room downstairs was haunted.

One night, my parents were at the Legion, Libby was staying with friends and I was drifting off to sleep, when the door to my room opened, scraping across the low plush carpet, letting in the light from the hall. I called out, "Mom, I'm awake," because I thought she'd returned and was checking in on me. But the door just closed and when I opened it, no one stood in the hall. I was alone in the house. I climbed back into bed and crossed myself over and over again. I was seventeen. I didn't pray anymore. Praying was a memory like all the other childhood games. *Holy Mary Mother of God. Three blind mice. Blessed art the fruit of thy womb Jesus. Three blind mice.*

But even as a teenager, the sign of the cross still had the

power to soothe me. After this first experience, I was ready whenever the ghost showed up, rosary wound around my fist, a glow-in-the-dark statue of Mary at my bedside.

My nightlight used to flicker like the flame of a fire and make the sound of a dragonfly's wings. My uncle Horst, who was an electrician for the public school board, came over and fixed it. Just a short. But it happened again. And again.

In the morning, I go for breakfast with Mom and Auntie Nelly to Smitty's in Kingsway Garden Mall. I ask them if they remember the ghost because I know they do.

"That thing with the light was weird," Nelly says. She's my mom's older sister, but her face is still girlish. Long lashes lap at her brows when she blinks.

Mom perks up. She's having one of her bad days. Her right eye is weepy from surgery. It squints and puckers. It looks like a leaky belly button. Her left eye is bright blue. "There are many ghosts in our family. When Baba saw your gido after he died in the car crash, all her own kids thought she was dreaming or nutty, including your dad. You were still a baby when your grandfather died, you wouldn't remember, but that summer we all drove out to Saskatchewan for the funeral. We stayed on the farm with her and one day I asked her about what she'd seen. She said the night after he died, she was lying in bed, couldn't sleep, when suddenly she felt the room go cold."

We all lean in closer, huddle together in the busy restaurant. I have a chill. I pat down the hairs on my arm. An ambulance drives by. Its lights flash. The restaurant noises seem to get louder, cups clinking, knives scraping, people talking. We compete against the wail of the siren, which stops just outside the mall's door. The paramedics walk in and people hush. We crane our necks, but can't get a good look at what's happening. Nelly half stands up. "It's an older gentleman. Must be a heart attack. I don't think he was choking. They're listening to his chest. Putting him on a gurney." She sits back down. The people at the surrounding tables avert their eyes, smile weakly as their breakfasts arrive. The ambulance sits outside for a while before driving away. I'm thinking in Top Five lists again. Top One place I wouldn't like to have a heart attack: Smitty's Restaurant in Kingsway Garden Mall during the breakfast rush.

We came here because my Auntie Nelly still thinks of Smitty's when she thinks of me. When I baked pies for the restaurant, I was allowed to bring extras home. At Thanksgiving, there was always a surplus of pumpkin pies, and my parents would invite all the aunts and uncles and cousins over for a treat. Nelly nudges my side with a plump elbow and promises, "After breakfast we'll treat ourselves to a slice."

Our food comes. The smell of sausage and eggs wafts over our table. My waffle is covered in fake whipped cream and half-frozen berries. I pour artificial maple syrup over the plate. Our cups are refilled and the coffee is so weak I can see through it. I could weep. Seriously. I haven't cried once since I got the phone call from the doctor, but now it seems like any small disappointment is enough to make my throat tighten and my eyes go wet. I tear the soggy waffle apart with my fork.

"What about Baba and Gido?" I ask, now only half-heartedly interested in ghosts.

Mom answers quietly, "Baba woke up and it was cold. She was going to get an extra blanket and there was Gido, standing at the foot of her bed."

"Then what?"

"She said she could tell that he just wanted to let her know everything was going to be OK."

"And that was like the ghost you saw, right?"

Mom nods. "Same thing happened to me. That's why I wanted to talk to Baba and let her know she wasn't seeing anything that wasn't there."

Nelly adds, "It was our Uncle Cliff, wasn't it?" She looks at me and explains, "Uncle Cliff was a real mean bastard. Whipped his kids. I think there was some sexual abuse happening, too. That side of the family's a little funny. Simple. We're really only once removed from white trash." Nelly frowns. "He used to set the neighbours' barns on fire." She closes in, her fork marking the air with punctuation. "One day he went into his own barn with a shotgun and blew his head off as he dropped a lit match on the dry straw. I tell you, he was a devil. I didn't want to see him when he was alive, never mind dead."

"How'd it happen?" I ask Mom.

"Just like Baba." She takes a napkin and mops her weepy eye. "Dad was working the night shift and I woke up to a freezing cold room. I sat up in bed and there was Cliffy Mactavish. I recognized him immediately. He raised his hands, palms upward, and I knew he was asking forgiveness for all the bad he'd ever done."

"What'd you do?"

"I forgave him the best I could."

I push my plate back and drink my too-sweet coffee. "Why'd he come to you? He didn't do something to you, did he?" My mom shakes her head and shrugs. I look at her and know why. Because my mom is the rare person who can tell you everything is going to be fine and you believe her. She has the power to reassure. She has the power to bless.

We argue over who will pay the bill. My mom wins, or loses, depending on how you look at it. Uncle Bart, Nelly's husband, is watching golf on TV with my dad when we come home. I didn't see him when he dropped Nelly off for brunch earlier. Now he glances at me. "Well," he says.

"How are you?"

"Long time."

"Yeah. How's retired life?"

"Good, good."

I sit on the floor and our attention shifts to the TV. Tiger Woods misses a putt. "Ha," Uncle Bart gloats. "Damn spook."

I'm not sure I heard correctly, but my mom cautions, "Baaaart."

Uncle Bart grunts. He looks at me. "A Ukrainian and a Pole were walking down a country road. The Ukrainian starts walking strangely."

I smile. This is the joke he used to tell me as a child.

"The Pole says, 'What's wrong?' Ukrainian says, 'I have to go to the bathroom.'" Bart would hold up two fingers and whisper, "Number two." I'd giggle. "'Go in the bush,' says the Pole. 'I don't have any toilet paper,' says the Ukrainian. 'Use a buck,' says the Pole. So the Ukrainian goes into the bush, comes out a few minutes later, but is still walking funny. 'What's with you?' says the Pole. 'Have you ever tried wiping yourself with three quarters, two dimes and a nickel?'" Bart'd pick me up and tickle me until I cried and my panties were a little damp from pee.

"Hey, that joke doesn't work anymore," I say. "You know—now that we've got loonies instead of dollar bills."

Bart doesn't say anything. He stares at me and then looks back to the TV. When he leaves, I notice his leg is turned inward and he winces as he stands. "Gout," my dad sighs into my ear.

Dad gives me twenty dollars as I leave the house that night. "It's OK," I say, shoving the money back at him.

"Take it," he says gruffly. My parents have never had a lot of money, but what they have, they share. One time, I came home from babysitting pissed off because our rich neighbours gave me a ten and said I could come back with the dollar change I owed them. Cheap bastards. My mom told me that's why they were rich and we never would be.

◦ ◦ ◦

Friday night and I'm meeting Joe and a bunch of people at Dewey's Bar. My parent's still worry when I stay out late, so I've arranged to stay with Libby, who is back in town. I've been looking forward to this all week. Joe is anticipation, an unrealized dream that keeps me coming back for more. We keep each other in reserve so when things don't work out with other people, we can console ourselves with the idea that *we* could be together. We *could* be happy.

When I arrive, I see a table full of guys I used to know. There's Joe, Pepsi, Spaniard, Scramble, Tommy, Boston and Lush. Before there were some girls, but they've all left or gotten married. The boys look slightly bleary-eyed, but still manage to greet me with enthusiasm. I settle in and Lush, who's older than the rest of us, continues slurring his story. I never knew if they called him Lush because of his velvety, come-hither eyes or his alcoholic tendencies. I suspect the latter.

"Before I went to prison, this queer was sending me flowers and expensive gifts. My mom was worried I was hustling and kept bugging me about it. When the cops came and picked me up I said, 'See mother, I'm a thief not a whore.'"

I try to flag down the waitress. I have some serious catch-up to do if I want to be on the same level as these guys.

"'If someone tries to fuck you, fight 'em to the death' was my dad's final advice before they put me away. Jesus."

I buy a beer for me and a Bombay and tonic for Lush, who's still talking.

"Sent to the Big House. That's where I stuck myself for the first time. I was seventeen. Jesus. I shoulda never been put there. First-time offender. Jesus." He shakes his head, what a waste. "The last thing I wanted to be was a junkie—good thing the last thing I didn't want to be was a Volkswagen or someone'd be driving me right now."

The table falls silent for a second as the joke settles in and then Joe thumps Lush on the back. "You smart bastard." We move on to the Black Dog, the Back Street Vodka Bar, the Commercial, and finish up at the Rev. At the end of the night, I'm too drunk to drive, so Joe and I sit in my mom's car and kiss. There is nothing in the world like kissing your first love, even if it's years later.

Joe once tried to explain our connection. He toyed with the idea of reincarnation, but found the odds of actually rediscovering your soulmate again and again to be too staggeringly unlikely. I remember him carrying around a copy of *The Eolian Harp* and quoting Coleridge to me.

And what if all animated nature
Be but organic Harps diversly fram'd

That tremble into thought, as o'er them sweeps
Plastic and vast, one intellectual breeze,
At once the Soul of each, and God of all?

I'd listen, straining to catch the words like elusive butter-flies. Joe wrote it down for me with a note I still keep folded, worn and torn: We are all of one mind, of one soul—reflections and variations of one another. Sometimes these variations are so extreme, I imagine, that feelings of kinship with another are an impossibility—like a toe, for example, meeting an ear with utter disinterest. In those instances, however, when two people meet and connect and love and feel so utterly no longer lost in the world, perhaps they are like two fingers—say one from the left hand and one from the right—discovering their sameness. You and I.

Joe was a romantic. He was going places. He was bound for greatness—even if he had no real plan or ambition. Now he looks to the sky through the windshield and points. "Look, a farting star." A light streaks across the darkness and he breaks wind. He turns to me, "They are very rare, you know."

He makes me laugh. It's as simple as that. I'm in love all over again.

Joe worries that the time for greatness has passed. I can relate. In Montreal, I'd settled into settling. I had a job I didn't hate and an apartment I liked. I lived in a big city and I'd learned to speak French. I never worried about what would come next, until I got that phone call. Results abnormal.

My hospital time was short. For two days, I watched old women shuffle by my room, arms pumping at their sides, dog-paddling air. They favoured nighties with ruffles and bows, while the male patients couldn't be bothered to change from their hospital-issued paper gowns. Crackling and crinkling, their flip-flops smacking the polished floor, the men peeked into my room as they passed. The women stared straight ahead. I slept a lot. On the third day, I was released.

I take Joe in my arms and feather his neck with kisses. I

suck on his lips and taste the juice of plums. We are sixteen, we are twelve, we are two, we are babies. My smooth thighs never get touched.

He proposes. "If we don't meet anyone by the time we're sixty, will you marry me?"

"Yes."

We fall asleep in the car and wake up cold. Early morning condensation beads the windows with droplets. I drive him home and then go to my sister's and quietly let myself in by the back door she's left open for me. The cats are sleeping. I curl up on the couch and try to sleep off the rest of my hangover. My tongue feels thick. I exhale rye. The sound of the neighbour's sprinkler lulls me to sleep. Tch Tch Tch Tch. Then double time, tchtchtchtchtchtchtch.

I wake up sweaty. The sun is burning a spot in my head and a cat is draped across my neck. Libby's already starting food for the barbeque. "Good morning," she says in a sing-songy voice. "Or rather, good afternoon."

"Hi." I take the two Tylenol and the big glass of cold water she offers. "You're my hero," I say.

She crinkles her brow. "I'm sure." She folds the quilt she put across me sometime in my sleep. I look around the house and make small sounds of approval. Her renovation project shows signs of slow progress. A window, half stripped of paint, reveals dark natural wood under layers of blue, white and eggshell. Plaster is torn from a wall that had to be redone due to water damage. I swing my legs off the couch onto new, used carpet. "If you buy it used, it won't give off the toxins that new rugs do," Libby explains. "Plus, I'm broke." She moves into the kitchen and I trail her, my head pounding. Too much alcohol and too much kissing.

My sister smells like lilies. I breathe through my mouth, feeling weak and shaky as I listen. "We took a pay cut at the hospital and the trip to Paris really sunk me into debt. But I have to show you my pictures. The tour was fabulous. I'd love to go again and actually spend some time there." She looks me up and down. "You look a bit wrecked. How was your night?"

"Good. Want me to do anything?"

"Naa, go ahead and take a shower. People will be here soon."

Mom and Dad arrive with Gizzy in tow and my sister's friends come bearing gifts. Catnip. Tins of Fancy Feast. A fake mouse. She thanks them and gets them settled with a drink. I've made a pitcher of rum cocktail with fresh limes and mint. Everyone accepts a glassful, but this is one of those "No, I couldn't possibly have another" kind of crowds. The guests consist of three sisters who Libby travelled to Australia with after they all graduated from university and Libby's best friend, Pam, a tall, buxom woman who wants to have a baby. "I can feel it, the clock running down. Tick. Tick. Tick," she explains while I stare at her cleavage. "But first, I have to find someone to marry." She takes a gulp of her rum punch.

I quickly put the thought of kids from my mind and focus on the attraction of marriage. One late night at my parents', I had a kind of revelation as I watched a comedy bit on TV by Dennis Miller, whose basic message was—Wake up, loser. You want to be alone all your life? What are you waiting for? So I'm thinking marriage might not be so bad, but I have no prospects. My relationships in Montreal are way too fleeting and insubstantial. The most likely possibility is Joe, but I'd have to wait over thirty years for the event, which actually might be worth it if we finally got to have sex after all this time. It's not like we don't want to have sex with each other, but we seem to be stuck in a habit of perpetual foreplay. I'm thinking maybe if we were married we'd be less afraid of disappointing one another. Of course, there's always the punk rocker turned folk singer, Alejandro Escovedo, but I'm guessing our brief exchange at the festival does not a marriage proposal make.

Besides, there are worse things than not being married. Right?

Look at my sister's friends. Career girls happily eating good food and chatting about cats until a big black thundercloud bustles in and breaks up the barbeque. "Was time to go anyway," Pam says, and the girls make a run for their cars with jackets pulled over their heads. Dad drives the truck up to the front of the house for mom and they're off with Gizzy panting on the window, making small puffs of white on the glass with each breath.

Libby and I do dishes after she tries to coax Ginger to eat some salmon, which she's carefully deboned. "Does she look all right to you?"

"Oh yeah, she looks fine. It's probably the heat." The cat is panting a little. I reach down and rub the sides of Ginger's mouth. Purr.

"So what's your plan?"

When someone from my family asks me this question, what I hear is, "Are you going to move back?" It makes me defensive. I lay it on the line. "I have a life there, you know. I get the impression that everyone thinks I'm still sleeping on a mattress on the floor. I'm an adult, you know. I have stuff. A box spring. A couch. Dishes . . ." I hear what I'm saying and picture my apartment.

I cleaned before I left. Two fluffy white towels hang in the bathroom. A print of a pastel landscape decorates one wall. The bed is made with tight, tucked corners. It could be a hotel room. Check-out time twelve o'clock.

Libby notices my silence. "I never meant anything by it," she says. "I know you have a life. I would hope so, you've been there over three years."

I look Libby in the eye. She stares back, clear green marbles. I hate it when she's sincere. I hate it when I misunderstand. My sister's always been the "responsible one." She's only thirty and is already saving for her own retirement. On weekends she goes to my parents' and helps them with odd jobs—weeding the garden, cleaning out gutters, shoveling snow—things my mom used to help my dad with before getting sick, things my dad used to be able to do alone, things I can't do because I'm far away in Montreal. I'm the "baby" of the family and I feel like it when I compare myself to Libby.

"I'm sorry. I seem to revert back to childhood when I come here," I say. "You know mom and dad still won't let me have a key to the house. They remember every time I lost them and every stupid thing I did. They hide it above the garage door for 'safekeeping.'"

Libby wipes the counter. "They're proud of you, you know. You did something they understand, you moved away from a small place that was suffocating you and started your own life."

She's watching Ginger, wet rag hanging from her hand. "Did you ever want to do that?" I ask.

She looks at me like she's just remembered I was there and pooh-poohs my questions with a wave of the rag. "I like it here."

"It's hard being away, you know. Nobody tells me anything. I didn't even know about mom's eyes until months later. You gotta tell me things." My voice rises. "You really have to tell me things."

Libby's gaze slides from mine and she wipes the counter again.

"What?" I ask.

Libby shrugs. "Nothing," she says, and then faces me again. "Mom says not to worry you. There isn't anything you can do. They are getting older, you know. They're going to die sometime."

"Mothers mortal? Next you'll tell me Santa doesn't exist." I'm trying for a joke but feel very unfunny. "Look, the fact is, I know mom's sick so I'm worried all the time anyway. It'd be nice to know exactly what I'm worrying about. I also know you do a lot for them. They depend on you. I feel guilty. I should be here. I even think about moving back for a year or two."

"What do you have to feel guilty about?"

"For everything. For moving away. For not coming back. For not being here for you."

"God, you really are like Mom."

"What do you mean? What does she have to feel guilty about?"

"Nothing in the world, like you. But she still does."

"Oh."

Libby picks up Ginger, and we go snuggle into the couch and watch a video. We choose a movie from my sister's large collection of Disney cartoons, fantasy flicks and romantic comedies. We watch *Battlestar Galactica* and Libby falls asleep with her favourite cat nestled contentedly in her arms. Ginger looks at me, blinking slowly. Her breath is laboured. Her sides shudder when she inhales. Since I've been sick, it is seems sickness everywhere. It's like you join a secret club. The membership fee is costly and, in the end, all you get is a hyperawareness of the fragility of life. I look away from Ginger and remind myself that I'm getting stronger everyday and that most people around me are fine: Libby, Joe, Penny, Nelly. With each name I feel a little better. "Healthy as a horse," my dad likes to say as he punches himself in the chest.

The next day, Libby and I visit our cousin Victoria in her new house. "Five bedrooms," Vicky says. "And look." We enter the living room and I can't stifle my gasp of shock. She smiles. "It's too big, isn't it?" We all stare at the immense television looming in the corner. "It's the biggest one they had. We paid over $5000 for it. The next day I had to take out more insurance on the house." She clicks it on. The hum of electricity fills the air.

"Derek loves it. It's his baby," she says.

"He's not back from the wedding yet?" Libby asks.

"Anytime now." Vicky turns off the TV and we go to the kitchen for tea.

"Why didn't you go?"

"Had to work and I really didn't want to drive to Calgary to go to a wedding of one of his second cousins twice removed that I don't even know. Margaret, Derek's mom, was a little put out. She likes to have the whole family around her, but sometimes you just got to put your foot down."

"HmmMmm," Libby and I hum in unison like we know what it's like to put your foot down to your mother-in-law.

Libby gets up to go to the washroom and Vicky leans con-spiratorially close to my ear. "We all wish she would find some-one." She plops down in the chair by my side and drops her voice to a lyrical whisper. "You," she says, pauses for dramatic purposes and brings the back of her hand to her mouth, the diamond of her engagement ring pressing against her lips in a soft kiss. She touches my arm. "You," she says again, "I have the feeling you're about to meet the man of your dreams." She has just given me her highest benediction. Her hand is cold. I gen-tly pull away.

"How's work?" Libby walks towards the table. Her nylons rub together, playing a tune of swish, swish. Steam from the tea coils in the air, blurring the powder blue decor of the kitchen. Libby and Vicky, who's a nurse too, exchange hospital stories.

"I can tell the sex of the baby before its head is out. I don't know how, but I'm always right," says Vicky. They continue relating incidents involving pus, urine, blood, stools, stones and other such niceties. It shouldn't really bother me, considering I shovel guts off the highway for pay, but for some reason there is a difference between gore that still lives and gore that's been long dead.

I've only once come upon a deer that'd just been hit. It was still breathing, but I could see its guts spilled onto the road, glistening in the glare of my headlights. I shut off my truck and heard the deer moan. The sound was utterly human and was the last the animal made. I waited for the body to cool. Mist rose from the dark hole in its stomach.

Vicky fixes me with a stare. "Do you brush your tongue?"

"Ahh, sure, I guess, sometimes."

"Derek smokes, right?" Libby and I nod. "Well, this week he went to the dentist. The guy hands Derek a mirror and pushes down his tongue. At the back of Derek's throat there are thick strings of black goop hanging, like something you'd find in a sewer."

"Yuck." I rub my queasy stomach and, through the thin material of my tank top, my fingers trace the slightly raised ridge of my scar. I stare at Vicky's glass shoe collection on a shelf above the table. Little slippers, twinkling colours, lined up in a row waiting, just waiting to turn pretty young girls into princesses.

◁◎ ◎▷

On Monday, Libby goes back to work so I return to my parents'. My vacation is almost over. I know the last couple of days will be the hardest. I don't want to say goodbye. But I do have to get back to work. In the fall, as the weather turns colder and there's less traffic, my job slows down, but all the student workers return to school, and someone is still needed for the odd accident. Besides, physically, I'm getting better.

I go for a run in the river valley to try to sweat out some stress. After the operation I couldn't climb stairs for a month. I had to learn how to pee again. The doctor suggested Kegel exercises to strengthen the pelvic muscles. Squeeze, release. Squeeze, release. I walked gingerly around my apartment, holding one hand on my stomach, the other on my back. I got groceries delivered and watched soap operas. "I feel like an old woman," I told my doctor. "I'm too young for this to happen."

She replied the obvious, "No, you aren't."

This is my first run since leaving the hospital. I plod. I jog so slowly, I can't even frighten the rabbit sitting at the edge of the trail. His soft brown face is encouraging. When I look back, his chubby bunny buns bounce off into the bush. I decide he is definitely a sign of good luck and pick up my pace. I pass an old man on the trail who looks into my eyes and cries out, "Bravo." Another good sign? I manage to sprint the last block home. Libby is on the phone.

"Hey, what's up," I pant into the receiver. I should have waited to cool down.

"Will you drive Ginger-cat and me to the vet in the morning?"

"Sure. Is she OK? Something wrong with your car?"

"I don't want to drive." Libby's voice softens, and Dad is doing the dishes, so I have trouble hearing her. "I made an appointment to put her down."

"What?"

"I told her last night to just go ahead and die. That it was all right, we've said our goodbyes, just go. But this morning she was still alive and she can't breathe and I can't watch her suffer like this."

I taste her tears in my throat. "What's wrong with her?"

"Leukemia. I knew it. Just like Buddy. They really go fast. You'll take me?"

"Of course I'll take you. What time?"

"Nine."

"Can I do anything? Want me to come over?"

"No." Then thinks again. "You can pray that she goes tonight."

Libby wanted to be a nun, even though my parents were lazy churchgoers, only attending mass on Christmas Eve. Every Sunday, Libby would get up early and walk by herself to church. My sister gave me my first rosary. She also gave me *The Outsiders*.

Libby and I would curl up on my bed and take turns reading the story to each other. *When I stepped out into the bright sunlight from the darkness of the movie house, I had only two things on my mind: Paul Newman and a ride home.* I had a crush on every boy in the book. I wanted to be Cherry Valance, but *I* would say "hi" to Ponyboy in the school hallways, no matter if he was a greaser. We always had a box of Kleenex close by for when Johnny dies. And after Dally is shot in the streets, I would imagine being there to hold his hand and kiss his eyelids. Salty tears on my lips. It's OK, everything's going to be all right.

◖◗

That night, I go over to Joe's for comfort, but Tommy and Pepsi are already there with a big baggie of pot. I wanted to spend my last night with Joe quietly, alone, my head nestled in his armpit, but the boys have settled in for the night, so I take the joint and inhale too deeply. The smoke burns my throat. Joe pounds my back. "Tell her about the cow." Joe passes the joint to Tommy.

"What cow?" I ask.

Tommy squints as he takes a drag. "It's a cow at school."

Joe explains, "He takes agricultural studies."

"There's a small farm outside the city as part of the program." Tommy stubs out the joint in a beer bottle cap.

"My mom used to work there," I say.

Pepsi pipes in, "I go there, too."

"So the cow?" I nestle into Joe's armpit.

His voice resonates loudly in the ear I have pressed close to his chest. "It's the craziest fucking thing."

Tommy nods. "This cow, that's part of our studies, has a hole in one of its stomachs. They have four, you know."

"That's too bad." I feel sluggish.

"No, you don't understand. It has a hole *cut* into its side so that students can open it up and put their hands inside the cow's stomach and feel around."

Voices gather around me. I close my eyes and try to imagine plunging my hand into a cow, but can only see a field full of cattle as if watching them from a car window. When I was young, my dad used to honk the horn at cows by the road and we'd all *moo*.

"Why haven't I heard of this? I go there too."

"I don't know."

I wonder what a stomach would feel like, what *my* stomach feels like. Squishy like peeled grapes? Warm? How was it with the doctor's hands inside of me? Was it like indigestion or was it a soft, intimate caress? I don't know. For the whole operation, I was a sky-blue ceiling gone black.

"How do you open and close it?" The boys are still talking.

"There's a cap."

"A cap?"

"Like a gas tank."

"Is there a key?"

"Hey, has anyone seen the key to the cow? Who was the last person to use the cow?"

"What do you mean—are there keys to the cow?"

I open my eyes. Wet my lips. "Like a gas tank, you know."

Pepsi sits with his head resting heavily in his hands. "I go there, too, why haven't I ever heard of the cow?"

Joe shifts, making me hit my chin against my chest. My neck cracks. I pull myself out of the couch to go pee. In the bathroom, I sit on the cool toilet seat and crane my neck to look out the high window that overlooks a garden. A breeze drifts in and I remember another garden full of beans, zucchini, lettuce—everything practical, except for one bush at the edge that blossomed yellow with lady's slipper flowers in the hottest days of August. When I was young, my mom would give me a salt shaker and send me through the rows of vegetables to hunt for slugs. While she and Baba pulled weeds and turned soil, I would carefully lift beet leaves and brush aside carrot tops to look for the slimy creatures. When I found them, I'd sprinkle salt on them and watch them writhe and curl into themselves until they dropped from the vegetables to the ground, leaving only a dark wet spot behind them.

The summer my baba died, the tomatoes hung ripe and heavy on the vine, dripping to the ground, forgotten. One night, just before Baba moved from our old house to the nursing home, we were woken by a high-pitched squealing. I ran outside and followed the sound to the lady's slipper bush, where I found the neighbour's cat shaking a squirrel in its mouth. I called for my mom to come. The cat proudly dropped its prey at her feet and my mom exclaimed that she had never before seen a white squirrel. Baba stood in her slippers on the back step, a shimmering pale shadow peering into the darkness.

As I bent to examine the animal, I saw a gash of red blood around the squirrel's neck. It lay quiet and still. My mom pointed to more blood on the ground and I realized that six tiny babies lay squirming in the dirt by the squirrel. When I saw those babies, I vowed to save them and raise them as my own.

Mom said they were too young and wouldn't be able to survive without their mother, but she gave me a shoebox lined with an old towel to serve as a crib for the orphans. When I showed my baba the little pink babies she nodded, her wispy hair trembling in the wind, and said it was a sign.

The little squirrels died within two days of their birth despite my constant vigilance and careful ministrations. I was surprised. I'd been convinced they would live. When my baba died, it seemed as though no one was surprised. After all, she was eighty-nine and she had been ill for over a year. But I think now, that perhaps her death had been a surprise—not for others around her—but for Baba herself. I picture my baba waking up with the sudden realization that she was no longer alive, an awakening and most profound sleep at the same time.

I rub my eyes and shake my head. I feel tired and older and stupid for sitting in the bathroom for so long. I reach for toilet paper and discover there is none. But there is a small basket filled with coffee filters, which I assume are to be used as a replacement. It works quite well. I wander to the kitchen for a glass of water.

"What do you think is the ugliest part of the human body?" Pepsi asks.

"It's all beautiful," I say, resting my back on one side of the doorway and my feet on the other. I wedge myself in between and shimmy to the top of the doorway where I look down on the boys. I haven't done this since I was a kid. I'm astonished I still can. "What do *you* think is the ugliest part of the human body?"

"The underside of the tongue," Joe asserts. He curls his tongue back, catching the tip under his front teeth, exposing moist lumpy red flesh shot through with fat purple-blue veins, and I have to agree that this is the ugliest part of the human body.

Pepsi and Tommy stumble out the back. They live closeby, just down the alley. Their debate continues into the night. "Toes are for sure uglier than balls."

"Depends on the balls."

Joe closes the door and asks me to stay the night, and I would like to climb into bed, onto him, escape into sweat and sweet kisses. But sweet kisses are no longer enough. I tell him I should go home so I can get up early and take Libby to the vet's. I think he is relieved.

Even though it's late and there is no traffic, I drive carefully, meticulously. I'm not really high anymore, but I have to fight to focus on the road because my attention is too easily swayed by a shiny new garbage can or a garden gnome.

I pull into the driveway at a perfect angle, fish the key from the hiding spot and go directly to my room. I no longer stay downstairs. The haunted room is now used for extra storage: sweaters in summer, sandals in winter, my old music box collection, bundles of dried flowers, an ancient black and white TV, and a ghost.

I sleep on what used to be Libby's bed in the room next to my parents'. It's very narrow. I have to be careful to be quiet. I slide my hand down my panties. This is the first time since my operation. I'm nervous. What if it doesn't work? Gizzy crawls from under a chair, whines a little and hops on the bed. "Shhh." I press my finger to my lips. She settles down by my feet, her soft, furry butt pressed against my feet. I stop. I can't do this with an audience. She closes her eyes and falls asleep. I wet my finger and my hand drifts down. I come quickly, fervently, repeatedly. Without a sound.

In the morning, the birds outside scold a squirrel, who scolds them back. I'm precariously close to the edge of the bed and wake up with a jerk that almost sends me to the floor. Bed is the only place I want to be right now, but the clock shines 8:04 so I get up and get dressed. Outside, my dad's already in his office smoking. The tip of the cigarette glows hot in the windowless garage. When my dad inhales, he looks like a Cyclops with one tiny red eye. Though I swore off smoking after Vicky's story about Derek's blackened throat, I'm dying for a cigarette. I get into the car and chew my nails all the way to Libby's.

"You're early," she says, clothed in a long shapeless dress of cotton. Her face looks swollen, her eyes lined with dark circles. "It only takes about ten minutes to get there and I don't want to make Ginger wait too long."

"Where is she?" I follow Libby up to her room, where the cat lies under a chair. I crouch down and put my hand out. Ginger closes her eyes and draws in raspy, hard-worked breaths. When Libby puts Ginger in the carrier, the cat lies limply in her hands. I take off my sweater and tuck it around Ginger, trying to help, be useful.

Ginger is quiet on the ride over. I would prefer indignant howls, but all we hear is Ginger's struggle for air, which stops every so often. During these silences, Libby and I also stop breathing. The air conditioning hums. With my hands placed carefully on the steering wheel at two o'clock and ten o'clock, I can smell my sour sweat.

At the vet's office, we are immediately shown into a private room. I ask Libby if she'd rather I stay or go. She shrugs, so I stay. A woman in a white lab coat enters. She strokes Ginger's head. "She's not looking so good. You're doing the right thing," she says to Libby, who nods. I gulp. "You should know that this procedure is absolutely painless. Her brain is affected first, so all she will feel is the prick of the needle. She'll go fast, though, almost immediately, so if you want to say your goodbyes, you should do it now.

Libby's voice is sandpaper. "It's OK. We've already said our goodbyes last night." I pat Ginger's head and reach for the Kleenex.

The vet is speaking. "If you're ready, I'm going to get an assistant. You should know that at the time of death sometimes the animal will lose control of its bowels. Also, sometimes it is hard to get the needle into a vein at this point, so we may have to insert a catheter." Libby nods again. The vet returns with another woman in a shorter white lab coat who smiles gently and holds an electric razor. Together they shave a patch of fur off Ginger's front leg. The sound of the razor grates. The assistant searches for a different blade to get closer to the skin. Ginger's soft coat falls to the floor like fun fur. She lies perfectly still, her eyes trained on Libby.

A needle is produced which the vet tries to insert. When she is unsuccessful, she takes Ginger into another room. Libby and I wait. We wait so long, I begin to wonder if that's all. I look at Libby. She must know what is happening, but I lack the courage to ask. Just then, the vet returns. She lays Ginger on the table.

"Oh, I'm so sorry." She quickly grabs a cloth to wipe the cat's bloody paw.

"It's all right," Libby puts a hand out to Ginger. The vet puts the needle to the catheter, steps away from the table, and says, "She's gone."

Libby bends to kiss Ginger's head. I do the same. She smells like the sun. Her head is warm. My hair brushes against her paw and I come away with blood staining the tips of a few strands. Libby doesn't notice, so I hastily wipe the red away.

I turn to my sister and give her a hug. Her arms hang loosely at her sides, her body stiff, but I hold on and stare at the backs of my burning eyelids.

We get into the car and Libby says, "We can wait a little if you need to."

I swipe a hand across my damp face and attempt a little laugh. "If you wanted someone to be strong, you sure picked the wrong person to drive you. I cry at tampon commercials."

"It's OK. Everyone would have cried. Could you imagine Dad?"

We both smile. Dad is a notorious softie who used to take us to the movies and end up weeping. Both Libby and I remember walking out of *Where the Red Fern Grows*, each of us holding one of Dad's thick, strong arms. His eyes were a brilliant red, his hands clutching a crumpled hankie.

"Can you call Mom to let her know?" Libby opens the door and quickly catches Sebastian and Tookie, who both try to dash outside.

"Sure." I sit down heavily in the old stuffed rocking chair

my parents gave Libby, along with some other old furniture, to help fill up her house. Mom would always tell us how she used to sit in Dad's lap when they first met even though she was twice his weight. He would pull her into him, and the chair would rock and the springs would groan. By the time she was diagnosed with diabetes, she had already lost one hundred and fifty pounds, leaving only ninety-eight. Barely a lapful, really.

Once her insulin was regulated, she started to gain back weight. She followed the prescribed diet closely and growing up, I remember her as healthy and strong, even though the risk of comas, convulsions and blindness always lingered.

I've never been good at giving my mom bad news. I dial my parents' number slowly. She answers on the first ring. "Hi, Mom, it's me."

"Is Libby all right?" Mom is stuffy-nosed quiet. There has been a death in our family.

"She's doing OK. I'll stay here a while. We're going to watch some movies and take a nap. She has to work the night shift."

"You're coming home after?"

"Yes." I leave tomorrow.

"All right dear, we'll see you later."

When Libby and I part in the evening, we know it will be another couple of years before we see each other again. When I first moved, it seemed hard to leave the home I'd built for myself. But, oh, it is so much harder to leave the home I was born into. This time when I hug Libby her arms go around me, tight. Her body is soft and we don't let go for a long time.

I press my hand into Libby's. "It was on my sweater," I explain. She smiles down at one of Ginger's whiskers.

"Thanks, I'll add it to my collection." She has test tubes filled with whiskers. Since she was young she would find them everywhere. Gifts.

◀◉ ◉▶

My parents are eating dinner when I arrive. The smell of fried onions makes my mouth water. I go to the stove and fill my plate with perogies and onions and sour cream.

"She's OK?" Mom asks.

"She's OK." I cut the perogies with my fork and shovel the soft cheesy dough into my mouth. I feel starved. My dad happily refills my plate.

"I can cook up some more. Or there's some meatloaf in the fridge I could heat up," he says. Since I've been home, my mom and dad have kept the fridge filled with my favourite foods.

"No, I'm fine. Do you guys want to play some cards after dinner?"

"Sure."

The sky glows amber and then darkens to a deep electric blue. None of us want to watch TV, so we play progressive rummy at the kitchen table. We sit in a circle and Dad deals the cards slowly, snapping each to the table. When he gives me two cards at once, he licks his thumb to separate the cards. "Dishpan hands," he jokes.

Mom drinks a glass of wine, saying, "What the hell." She adds cola and ice to her glass. We eat wheat crackers, orange cheddar cheese and pre-sliced dill pickles. Usually, these snacks are brought out for special occasions like Christmas or the Super Bowl, but I suppose tonight, too, is a kind of celebration. We are drinking to our last night together, but the room is not festive, the air is already too heavy with goodbyes.

"We should have played a penny a point. Dad could have bought you dinner," I say after Dad beats us three times in a row.

Mom shakes her head. "I won't play for money. When we play partners with the neighbours, they want to play for money, but I always say no way."

Dad collects the cards with a groaning sweep of his hands. "They're not very good," he says confidentially.

"And they cheat." Mom turns from the sink where she's rinsing our dishes. Her hair is pushed in on one side from the nap she had earlier. Grey streaks the centre. It looks like a wildflower has been attached to her head.

"How do they cheat?"

"Lay down a wild card or an out card by accident and then pick it up again." Mom points in Dad's direction. "He's good at calling them on it, but when he was in the hospital, I could never win a game. So we stick to our guns, as they say, and never play for money."

My stomach slowly sinks to the ground, a puddle at my feet. "Hospital?"

"When he had the heart attack."

My dad looks down. Mom turns back to the sink, busying herself with the clean dishes. After a long silence, it is obvious they won't say anything. I feel my frustration rise.

"How could you not tell me? My god, you had a heart attack. *You?*"

"I'm fine. It was minor. We didn't want to worry you."

My knees quiver under the table. I stare at my feet. My sparkly blue toenails seem ridiculous. I look into my dad's face and see all trace of laugh lines and dimples has fled. His dentures click. His hands lie crumpled on the cards.

I curl my toes under. "Are you fine now?"

Mom sighs into an open cupboard. She closes the door and turns to me.

"He's really fine."

"I'm really fine. It was minor. They kept me for a little longer to take a good look. They could never get me to the doctor before, so once they had me, they had to do the whole work-up."

Mom joins us at the table and I ask, "Will you tell me next time something happens to either of you?"

"We don't want to worry you," Mom says. Dad's hand comes awkwardly off the cards and onto my arm. He squeezes once. When he pulls away, the ghost of his fingers remains.

What could I say to my parents? I haven't told them about my own illness and was evasive during my whole visit. When Penny called to invite me over and my mom asked why I didn't go, I told her I was tired. And it was true. It takes a lot of energy to keep avoiding your own thoughts. I think now that maybe I should have gone to meet Penny's children. At least then, they would seem real to me. My mind is already too full of babies that exist only in my imagination. Like phantoms, they visit me in the middle of the night and I wake up cold.

I think of the last weeks I spent alone in my apartment, pretending everything was normal while carefully avoiding the thin red slash across my abdomen. I imagined my stomach hollow, an empty jug. And I heard plainly the sound of that vessel when a strong wind blew—a low, steady howl.

Mom stands up. "Time for me to hit the hay, as they say."

"Me too," my dad says.

"Can I take the car out for a drive? I won't be long."

"Sure." Dad tosses me his keys. I see the key for the house on the ring and grin, matching Dad dimple for dimple.

"I'll lock up behind me." My mom stops me at the door. She kisses my forehead twice. Her lips are moist and my forehead feels cool like when Libby would touch holy water to my skin before entering the church. Blessed. She moves away and Dad rests his hand lightly on the small of her back as they walk towards their bedroom.

The night warms me as I step from the air-conditioned house. I open all the windows in the car and tour the city. Joe's place is dark. It's a ground-floor apartment, so I tap on his bedroom window. He blinks sleepily and I kiss his smile goodbye for now. Driving through my old neighbourhood, I startle rabbits in the ravine as I pass. On my way out of town, I see the hospital where I was born. Libby works there now. Silent byebye.

When I reach the highway, I merge into empty lanes. The road is flat and straight, slicing the fields of wheat I can't see but can smell. The sky is moonless. The wind clamours around my head. My thoughts complain they can't be heard. The better for me —I say to my thoughts—the better for me. I touch my forehead, chest, shoulder and shoulder, and reach to the dash to turn out the headlights.

I'm driving. Joe and I used to do this on ut then everything was washed in a silvery ed the way. Tonight, the darkness is complete. the windshield, trying to see something besides ck hurts. If I had wings, this is what it would feel e them ripped off.

nic, fumble for the headlights. Night is hitting my eyes ne wind. I ease my foot off the accelerator and depress the ke. The back of the car tries to catch up to the front in a wing dance. When I finally find the lights, the beam cuts into a farmer's field and I am sitting close to the ditch at a crooked angle. My teeth chatter. I lean my head against the cool window and listen to the crickets sing. Tomorrow won't be the sky, the plums, the smell of sweet grass.

My mom always said that having me changed her life in more ways than one. There were complications during the delivery. Mom says that when she had me, she died. It was only for a minute, but the doctor couldn't find a heartbeat and had to pound her chest to bring her back. "Back from where?" I used to ask. And Mom would smile and rock me in her arms and hold me a little closer.

"I can't tell you that," she'd shake her head. "But I do know it. I was only there a short time, but it was long enough to know." I would listen to her voice and press my back closer to her chest, craving her heat more than her answer.

august 2005

Born and raised in Edmonton, Alberta, M A R C I Ð E N E S I U K has crossed this country several times by train, as well as travelling through Canada, the United States and Mexico by motorcycle. She has an MA in Creative Writing from Concordia University and has taught at Seneca College, UQAM and Concordia. She currently lives, works and writes in Montreal.